Vaporfornia

By Robert Stark

Edited by Matthew Pegas

and cover illustration by Mark Velard

Vaporfornia

By Robert Stark

Copyright © 2021

Printed in the United States of America

First Printing, 2021

ISBN 978-0-578-32185-1

"Robert Stark—as much a painter with words as a novelist—delivers, a surreal, imagistic follow-up to his 2017 classic *Journey to Vapor Island*. *Vaporfornia* offers a blunt vision of the decay of the California dream contrasted starkly with a bold vision for the future we could have had."

--Matthew Pegas, author of *Dragon Day.*

Chapter 1: Vapor Privilege

Take in another deep breath. The air is nice: warm and dry with a whiff of dry grass and pine. The sound of the songbirds and crickets as it approaches sunset. It's nice and all, but it would be great to have someone to share this romantic moment with. Yes, the perfect spot to take a date for a sunset picnic. Some girls say they like hiking but just end up staring at their iPhone the entire time and then complain about wanting to head back indoors. That sounds terrible. I know. Like some rightwing misogynistic jerk.

Forget about that. Just enjoy the tranquility of nature. I'd like to go to Yosemite this summer but I don't have a car and am short on funds, but that's ok because there's so much great wilderness to explore right here in my own backyard. Just be thankful some money-grubbing bastard didn't buy up all this land and cover it with McMansions for more corporate drones.

The crisp golden hills are dotted with oaks that give off a blueish hue this time of day. Some in groves with the rest spread out. Some of these trees must have been here when the first European settlers arrived. I learned in school that the golden grass was brought here by the Spanish Colonists. Maybe we should have indigenous plants instead and reject European colonization. But all the golden grass is just splendid. I just want to take off my clothes and roll around in the warm dry grass, even if it scratches up my back.

Looking out over Walnut Creek I can see my neighborhood in the distance. I can't believe I've hiked this far. One day I shall hike all the way to the summit of Mount Diablo. I remember when my uncle was still alive, before he took his own life, he would take me up to the summit. I felt like I was up on Mount Olympus with the gods.

On a clear day I could see to the City and the Sierras. I think it's the highest viewshed after Mount Kilimanjaro. I've got to save up to buy a car so I can drive up to the summit again. Maybe get a summer job. My dad keeps telling me to stop sitting around and go out and get a real job, become a real man who contributes to the capitalist economy. He doesn't really get it. He got into Tech at the right time and made great money but conditions have gotten worse for workers in this country, not just the proletariat.

Now that his company is laying off workers, especially older workers like him, he fears he will be laid off soon. He comes home every night, gets drunk and watches rightwing cable news pundits rant about how socialism is destroying the American Economy and then goes on about how immigrants are stealing our jobs.

You can't really blame immigrants. We live in a capitalist economy where all workers are disposable; brainwashed by corporations that they need to acquire material possessions in order to have any value as a person. That 20th Century model of getting a corporate job and buying an SUV and big house in the suburbs is so outdated. All this competition for money and status. For stuff we really don't need is destroying the planet.

Anyhow, back to me. Yeah, went through some severe depression in High School. Didn't really fit in with the popular crowd, repeated incidents of social rejection. Had a few friends but they were into your stereotypical nerdy interest. But I had bigger dreams. I could have gotten into a great university to study journalism. Started out getting good grades, straight A's in honor's courses, but then went through a phase of depression and I don't know if I can even afford college with all the student debt, even with some underpaying retail job.

But before you think I'm going to go crazy like that Noam in Connecticut. No way. I have a life to live and I'm going to make the best of it. I should head back for dinner soon. Let me take in one more breath of fresh air and watch the sunset highlight the golden grass.

Heading back to the trailhead, I unlock my bike and ride through our suburban neighborhood. There's a group of bratty teens, a few years younger than me skateboarding as their snotty blonde girlfriends watch. Are they sneering at me?

Sometimes I really just hate White people. Look I have White Privilege too. I know. Even though I'm not the most popular guy I get to live in a nice area and at least had the opportunities to succeed even if I didn't make the best of them.

I just think about all the poor people of color who don't have those opportunities. Yes, true. High School is over so I need to stop thinking about silly adolescent drama and social cliques. I have to prepare myself to be a leader, a journalist who fights for social justice to make the world a better place.

Finally home, dad's car is parked outside. Hungry from the long hike, my mom must be making dinner.

Oh shit! There's that girl next door. That cute blonde, Chloe. She was a Freshman at my high school last year but we never spoke. But sometimes we'd awkwardly exchange glances. Doesn't matter. She's way too young for you. You could get arrested for just looking at her.

Dad opens the door, "Max. Where have you been all day?"

"I went hiking up in the foothills," I respond.

He orders me to sit down. I protest, "look dad, I'm 18 now."

"As long as you live under my roof you answer to me," He responds.

My mom says "give him a break. He just graduated."

Dad bangs the table "stop wasting your life Max. What are your plans for the future?"

"I told you, I want to study journalism," I say.

He responds "oh, common get real. Step up. Take action for once and think of a career that will actually make you money."

I look away. Tired of another one of his rants.

"You're always complaining to your mom about which girl ignores you but if you want to get the ladies you need to start making money," my dad says.

"Knock it off, Mitch," says mom.

He responds "this is my house. I worked my ass off to pay off the mortgage."

My sister walks in disrupting another potential fight.

Mom says: "hi Stacey, dinner is ready."

Mom ordered some Indian take out. My personal favorite.

Dad complains "can't you make something decent for once, like steak? Not this Pajeet shit. All day at work. Always going on about bobs and vegana." I don't think I can take another one of his racist rants. I do love Indian food though; Palak Paneer, Lentils, Raita, Garlic Naan, and a Mango Lasse. All vegetarian. The Hindus are far more enlightened than us Westerners when it comes to how they treat animals. I remember this Indian girl in my health class. I feel bad and a bit racist for forgetting her name, but she gave the most moving speech on the horrors of factory farming and health benefits of veganism. Ever since then I've tried to stay the course even if I sometimes slip and have a bite of steak.

Dinner is awkwardly silent. Dad finishes his Lamb Vindaloo and goes back to watching his rightwing cable news show with some pundit ranting about how corporations need tax cuts and how we need to bomb Iran. Funny how capitalism conditions one to worship their oppressor.

I overhear my sister on the phone. Is she talking to a boy? She's entering high school, a freshman already talking to boys while I have spent my entire high school years alone and dateless. Don't get bitter and turn into another Noam. We are all on different courses in life. Yours is to enlighten humankind; show the world how to better treat their fellow beings by exposing them to the beauty that they've been deprived of. I've taken loads of photos of nature and architecture to submit to an exhibition at an art gallery in Berkeley. And all proceeds will go to a shelter for abused transgendered persons of color.

After dinner I go to my room to contemplate. I enrolled at the local city college, signed up for courses in journalism, broadcasting, political science, and photography. No, it's not

University but I will get over my depression, get good grades, transfer to a prestigious University, and go on to accomplish great things.

I stay up all night looking at my photos. Most of them of nearby wilderness. I need to take a trip to the City to get some urban photos. Beauty is unjust because it's a finite resource. But once I spread it to the world everyone will be equal and free.

In my sleep my mind tries to process all my photos and other images I found online. The visuals of the golden hills, neon lit cityscapes, and girls I like; both from school and from social media all blending together in my dreams. The gold from the hills, gold neon, and girls' hair all now just one blur of gold.

Whenever I dream, I can sense what I'm missing out on. Sometimes I see it vividly yet locked out, unable to touch or partake. The energy representing everything I so deeply desire surrounds me, yet I'm still alone in a dark bubble.

Chapter 2: The Oasis

The next morning my dreams become just another blur. The harder I try to remember the more I forget. To clear my mind, I take a Klonopin and go out to the kitchen to make some coffee. I've got the whole summer ahead of me. Can't waste another day indoors. Today I shall climb to the summit of Mount Diablo.

Excited, I quickly shower, get dressed, and take a few bites of leftover Indian food. I have not planned out how I will get to the summit but I have all day. I get on my bike and head off to the trailhead and start from there. At the trailhead there's an equestrian center. That girl in the riding uniform looks vaguely familiar. Have I seen her before?

I get another look at her face. No, but she's really cute. She rides off with her instructor as I head off on my own quest. After hiking through the foothills I reach the base of the Mountain. Looks way too steep to hike up. Every time I reach this point I get intimidated by the ascent.

I should have researched trailheads online. And I forgot to even pack water. Another day, when I'm prepared, I'll make it up there. Man, it feels like almost 100 degrees. Would be nice if they had a swimming hole up here. I look out and notice all the mansions with pools that dot the hillside. All those rich fuckers with their private pools. We should all have access to swimming no matter our class, race, age, or social status.

I take out my binoculars from my backpack. Looks like someone's having a pool party. I remember riding by that house on my bike and seeing their daughter being dropped off from cheer practice. I can vaguely make out the beige blobs of flesh in the pool. It would be nice if I could join them. I wonder if my neighbor's having another pool party this summer. Think about all the girls. When was the last time you even went for a swim? Better get in shape first.

I take in a deep breath, close my eyes and try to meditate. Just enjoy this beautiful setting and fresh warm fragrant air. There's no social status up here. We're all just one with nature and other Hippie stuff like that. A swift gust of wind nearly knocks me over. I open my eyes. Everything's so much more intense; the colors, the scents. All my senses feel alive. Before it was all just one blur. As if I was living in a simulation. Something about the power of meditation.

I check the time on my phone but something is off. The time's not working, numbers constantly changing. Let me check Google Maps to check my location. That isn't working either. Am I totally off the grid?

You don't need technology. Just be free in nature. Screaming from the top of my lungs, Max! This is your world! You are in control! Your visions are reality! All of a sudden, a jolt of energy hits me. The glittery gold of the hills becomes even more intense and my surroundings become larger. I run my hands through the grass. The blades sparkle as I touch them. I start running, feeling the forces pulling me in.

Looking out I see no sign of human habitation. Nothing but hills as far as the eye can see. But wait. Beyond the jagged glistening ridge I can make out a castle in the distance. I don't remember ever coming here but I've heard stories about the ruins of some cult leader who claimed to tap into the supernatural powers of the subconscious. Rumor has it he had a watering hole where his teenage concubines would swim nude. Anyhow his entire compound was burnt to the ground by the parents of the teens, but this looks intact.

As I run towards the castle, I'm no longer out of breath, with unlimited energy. I must see if I can climb up to check out the view. There's a spiral staircase that leads up to the top. It's more of a watchtower than it is the kind of castle one would reside in. I quickly climb up to survey my domain. Out over the golden hills this magical light nearly blinds me.

Looking closer, while squinting my eyes, I can make out something masked by the glowing golden light: a small body of water amidst the woodlands. I can even hear laughter in the distance. The waterhole. It's still there! Just like in the old photos I've seen online.

The disorienting spiral staircase down causes me to totally forget the direction of the waterhole. Too restless to check again from the watchtower, I head off on the path, hoping it will lead me to wherever I need to go. Luckily, I feel this force of energy pulling me in the right direction, even as the pathway forks. Through a fragrant eucalyptus grove and then down into a canyon where the oaks condense along the creek where I can hear the sound of a rustling stream through the woods.

I've studied the geography of this area in depth and don't remember a stream in this area. And it's not just a trickle which is typical this time a year but rather a cascade. Walking through the woodlands I hear that giggling again. The stream must lead to where that sound is coming from.

Everything here has this enchanted scent, but not what is typical. Something more alluring that you would find at a theme park or resort but more natural; amplifying the scents that exist in nature into a perfume.

After jogging along the creek, I can hear the sounds of waterfalls and giggling. Climbing up this steep hill I should be able to view it from the top. I thought this was just some crazy hallucination, but this is real.

Whenever I would hike around these parts on a hot summer afternoon, I would always fantasize about taking off my clothes and swimming at sunset. But right there below me is the waterfall cascading down into a waterhole nestled in the woodlands. And it's packed with teens swimming.

Did I just hear my name? No way. Must be another Max.

Looking out I can see that there's a long body of water that curves around the hilly oak woodlands. The sun is starting to set but there's a sparkling light illuminating the water and golden grass, with mist rising up as the air cools off. Probably some exclusive resort or swim club. The kind of place that would exclude someone like me. So exclusive that there's no unaesthetically pleasing gate but you must enter through a secret camouflaged portal that I somehow managed to get through. Might as well be a portal to another dimension.

What matters is you got in and no asshole is going to kick you out. This is that place where you can just be in the moment and not daydream about what it could be or where you are going next.

I hear that giggling again, the voice calling "Max, come join us."

It has to be another Max or they're just playing some prank on the intruder who they've identified with facial recognition, but the voice does sound familiar. Regardless, I have to find out. Rushing down the other side of the hill as quickly as I can, I look out at the water. Right in front of my eyes, there's a bunch of blonde teens skinny-dipping.

I've never seen a pretty girl nude before, and the guys as well. As if you took a handful of the best looking and most popular students from my high school and multiplied them.

I look to see if anyone recognizes me but they're all too busy to notice the intruder. Anyways, I'm getting in. I take off my clothes but keep my boxers on to show some modesty. Watching the guys splash water on the girls, they'd better not get out in case I see their junk. I quickly jump in to join them. The water which comes up to my chest feels amazing.

Just relax Max and try not to stare at them. Perhaps they will invite you to join them. I dunk under the water and come up for air. Everything is just perfect here; the temperature, the way the water feels on my skin, and the all-around magical atmosphere with the illuminating lights, sound of the cascading waterfall, and scent of the woods with a whiff of campfire.

I could get used to this and never leave. The perfect vacation destination. Except I don't have to fly halfway around the world. If I can just figure out the exact GPS coordinate of the portal I can come here whenever I please.

I hear that giggling again and look around. That's her. That girl from my dreams. Perhaps she's some TikTok teen celebrity. Her image must be implanted in my subconscious. But this isn't a dream. I've never felt more awake.

She swims underneath the waterfall. Following her, I swim around the waterfall. There's a small cave but no sign of the girl. I duck under the waterfall and come back up on the other side. One of the guys notices me, shouting "it's him. Noam! Get that faggot!"

I turn around and see all the guys looking at me. Must be some misunderstanding. But they look like they want to kill me. I swim away from them but there's another group of guys running towards the water, alerted of my presence, and out for blood.

They take off their clothes to jump in the water, but I make sure to look away while I keep swimming. I dunk underwater again. When I get back up there's another group of guys swimming towards me and more on the sides jumping in.

One of them yells "that's him! He tried to rape her!"

Yes, trespassing is *exactly* the same as sexual assault. The belief of the 1% that private property has more intrinsic value than human beings.

One of them yells "I'll fuckin kill you Noam!"

They've got the wrong person, but I feel his guilt, as if my transgressions brought this upon me. One of them jumps out and grabs me. As I duck underwater more of them jump on me. I can feel a muscular bare chest rub up against my back. Another grabs my head and pulls me down underwater. Not able to hold my breath I open my mouth. No water rushing into my lungs No suffocation. Doesn't even feel like drowning.

I try to open my eyes but no one's there. Just darkness. That world that I thought was waiting for me. Gone. Too good to be true. Just lying on my back in a cold sweat. Must have gotten a bad flu and had another crazy dream. My vision is still a bit hazy, but I can tell something is off.

This isn't my room. No, you're just having a fever induced hallucination. As my vision becomes clearer it looks like some fancy retro hotel suite. Like one of those hotel towers near Union Square. It's pouring rain outside. Strange on a hot summer day. Perhaps I was drugged and some LGBTQ man took me off to his hotel suite in the City to be his toy, or worse some sadistic serial killer. Is this how it's all going to end? One brief taste of the good life before a long, agonizing death and then lights out.

Startled by a presence. That feeling you get when you wake up from a nightmare. With my vision fairly sharp I notice across from me is a blonde teen guy in a kimono with large aviator sunglasses, and a sullen expression as he sips tea. Maybe he's the one who purchased me. Some wealthy family wanted to be woke and purchased a slave for their LGBTQ son. At least it's not some creepy fat old guy in assless chaps.

I hear some footsteps outside and a woman crying. Perhaps he is one of the teens from the resort and he was used as a decoy to lure me in to be used by that creep outside.

A man with a British accent yells "Roger, you better not be in there!"

The boy, Roger pulls me aside and into the closet. Roger says that he found me passed out on his bed.

Once in the closet he whispers in my ear "you're the man from California." Just before I get a chance to respond he quickly puts his hand over my mouth. I peek out though the crevice in the closet and see two men pull out a screaming, naked woman. An aristocratic looking middle-aged man takes out some priest's garb and starts performing some bizarre ritual while the other man restrains her.

Roger shows me his snow globe and explains in his mid-Atlantic accent that he bought it as a souvenir on a trip to California. I can vividly see everything in the snow globe as if I was there; a neon boardwalk, art deco skyscrapers, golden hills, a ski lodge in a pine forest, some handsome surfer guy, and the blonde girl I saw at the waterhole.

Roger says, "I saw you there."

I'm bewildered. He explains that he saw me inside the globe and used a ritual from his father's spell book to summon me.

This can't be for real. I scream, "wake up!" He puts his hand over my mouth.

Feels so real, not like a dream. No, wake up! I feel the energy pulling me away. Roger screams "please! Take me with you!"

I find myself falling back into the abyss, consumed with feelings of anxiety and hopelessness. Then bright lights shine in my face. Honk!

"Watch where you're going punk!"

A truck swerves out of the way as I find myself in the middle of a wide street at night. As I get to the side of the street I notice everything is closed. Must be really late. The only person on the street is a sleazy overweight middle-aged man with a meth addicted sex worker. I feel my Klonopin wear off as the withdrawal symptoms onset. As I look for the bike rack a helicopter hovers down over me shinning its searchlight. My anxiety levels rise even higher.

I reach into my pocket to see if I brought my pills. Nothing. The chopper is still there hovering over me. Don't let it know you're aware you are under surveillance. I unlock my bike so I can head back home.

Across the street there's a white Cadillac Escalade. Are they part of some surveillance team? I've done nothing wrong. Perhaps it was all that research I did on that mass killer Noam. I once posted anonymously on this forum for Incels; Involuntary Celibates who admire Noam and advocated violence against the socially and romantically successful.

At first, I thought they were progressive because they wanted to dismantle social hierarchies but man was I wrong. Yes, a lot of us are disenfranchised because of the excesses of late capitalism but these morons blame all their social failings on women and people of color and post Roger Blackstone memes unironically.

I'm not one of them, just got bored and needed some dark humor, but one of the forum members went on a copycat killing spree and the site got shut down. The Feds must have kept track of all the IPs of the posters including myself. In this time of heightened security any alienated individual who fits the psychological profile and online footprint of a potential mass killer will be under constant surveillance.

I look up and the helicopter zooms away. No need to be paranoid. Hurry home and take your pills. As I ride home on my bike the Escalade pulls up alongside me. The helicopter is now hovering up above where I live. Probably some elderly busybody called the COPS about a person of color taking a stroll through our neighborhood. They are the ones truly under oppression by the police and I shouldn't detract from their struggle with my paranoid nonsense and White People's problems.

Chapter 3: Retracing my steps

The next day I can't even recall going to bed the night before. That often happens to me when I'm up really late. Let me think about what I did yesterday. I went hiking in the foothills, Roger Blackstone as a teenager, the guys at the swimming hole mistaking me for the killer Noam, and that girl from my dreams. I have nothing going on today, so I decide to retrace my steps.

Let me see. I first left my bike near the equestrian center by the trailhead and then picked it up at a bike rack near downtown. That doesn't even make sense. I have to find the general vicinity of the waterhole by figuring out the general direction to Mount Diablo from downtown.

After riding my bike in that general direction, I notice a castle themed tower at the gate of an exclusive residential community. Looks similar to the castle I saw yesterday.

I take out my phone and Google this area which is called Zephyr Ranch. Under Google Images I see the castle in the hills that was incorporated into the development and even the waterhole. But this area is all built up now into a subdivision. Not that many teens either, just lots of entitled old rich people exploiting people of color.

It was just another crazy dream and that's that but I'm curious to check to see if the waterhole is still there. I head over in the general vicinity of where I think the waterhole was. Down the hills and through another subdivision is a flood control channel where I remember the waterfall being.

I follow a trail along the channel, totally forgetting the direction. At the end of the channel is a flood control basin filled with discarded mattresses and shopping carts. Right behind such an exclusive community.

I don't think the geographic location of the waterhole matters. It's all fantasy. Whenever I go places, I always envision how they should ideally be. If I had the resources of Blackstone I would go to every one of these locations and transform them into my visions.

I head towards downtown to find a place for lunch. For a suburban downtown, Walnut Creek isn't all that bad. Downtown is actually fairly walkable, with a handful of historic buildings, new buildings designed to look retro, and some cool fountains and courtyards, as well as all sorts of new projects to retrofit downtown to be more walkable and urban.

Passing another construction site for a mixed-use project. Can't wait to see how they all turn out. Even if some of the new developments are a bit banal. While daydreaming, envisioning what the area will look like in the future, I notice right in front of a strip mall and parking lot are a group of older people protesting.

One of the protesters hands me a pamphlet. They're complaining about some proposed development, "The Blackstone Arcade" that would replace the nearby parking lot and strip mall. On the urbanist blogs these protesters are described as NIMBYs, which stands for not in my backyard. Usually older people of privilege who oppose any efforts to densify suburbia and any building higher than two stories.

The renderings in the pamphlet depict multi-leveled brick structures covered in ivy, with a series of paseos leading to a central atrium, a waterfall fountain, industrial themed external glass elevators with gears, skybridges connecting the buildings, an astronomical clock, bulb sign, and retro lanterns. A futuristic take on old 19th Century aesthetics, reminding me of somewhere I've been but can't quite make out.

While analyzing the details, I'm interrupted by an angry middle aged woman yelling on her megaphone, "Blackstone gets density bonuses and height exemptions for providing affordable housing but fills all his units with pretty 18 year old high school seniors with wealthy parents."

I take the other pamphlet against Blackstone's under-construction resort, "The Oasis," which would replace a golf course in the foothills near Mount Diablo with a ski lodge themed resort. All surrounded by restored oak woodlands. The swimming area would feature a series of waterholes and lazy rivers through the oak woodlands. There's even an Old West themed animated neon sign advertising it from the highway. Just like in my vision from last night.

Perhaps I did stumble upon that camouflaged portal to a better world. Even all the teens and that girl. Yes, she's the one from my dreams. The pamphlet also warns that Blackstone has some bizarre interest in that cult leader who created the original oasis and that Blackstone wants to tap into the powers of the subconscious to take power for himself. Is he accessing my dreams and implementing my desires into his luxury developments?

There's that ethereal quality that exists in the dream-world, and only aesthetic production can make that a reality. To be able to live in one's dream. But I could never afford one of his projects so why would my visions even matter?

As my environmental racism lesson taught me, aesthetics are a luxury for the White capitalist class and detract from more important issues such as climate change and ending pollution in low income communities of color. It doesn't have to be that way. I think aesthetics are a human right.

I walk further down towards the upscale outdoor mall. They're removing my favorite old fountain with a griffin and lions that dated back to the 80's and replacing it with more sterile minimalistic junk. At least Blackstone's projects are innovative.

Chapter 4: The Architect Aristocrat

After another night of dreaming, all of my visions from the oasis are just a blur. There's a real world out there to explore besides daydreaming.

I have a week off before starting classes so I think I'll spend the day in the City. I love the City but with homework and all I haven't been in a while.

Take some photos perhaps. Lots of photos. Upload them to my photo blog. Become the top architectural photo blogger in the Bay Area and display all my work at the trendiest galleries.

My mom drops me off near the BART Station and hands me $20, wishing me a fun and safe trip. If Blackstone gets elected and implements the basic income he promises, I won't have to depend upon my parents for funds but he's still a really bad guy.

I thank my mom for her kind gesture and head off on my adventure into urban civilization.

I look around the area near the BART Station and see the massive parking lot. What a waste. I heard there's plans for some kind of mixed-use community near the station.

I've been reading a lot of urbanist blogs lately and there's been an ongoing debate about whether to support Roger Blackstone, with some woke urbanists supporting Dave Cohen-Rodriguez. Blackstone really is the candidate who wants to put architecture and urban planning front and center. But at what cost?

I go to the ticket machine, but it seems broken. I look around for assistance but no one's of help. I feel really shitty about myself but I can't wait to get to the City so I just sneak through the turnstile. I'm a criminal now and if I get arrested they will get a search warrant to find out I posted that meme disrespecting the victims of the Connecticut Massacre with that smug overweight cartoon toad, that is practically the mascot for those incel creeps.

I must do something righteous to make up for this selfish act. Maybe give my $20 to a houseless person. Transgendered if possible, but then I won't have money for lunch.

That's ok. You must sacrifice for your privilege. While waiting for the train, I look out over downtown Walnut Creek towards Mount Diablo and then over to the hills to the west covered in trees and mansions.

I think about the attributes of this location I appreciate, from the nature to certain structures downtown and in nearby towns. Then I think about all the wasted space in-between. What if this all was condensed with Blackstone's proposals thrown in, and the wilderness was reclaimed from sprawl? There are pieces everywhere spread out but something is missing in the spaces in-between. I think that's what those crazy dreams have been trying to tell me.

Finally, the train arrives. Cool 70's Retro Aesthetic but a bit rundown from lack of maintenance. It's not too crowded but I don't want to sit down. There's a lot to see from the train.

"Next Stop Lafayette."

Lafayette is a ritzy town, part of the affluent Lamorinda region, comprised of the towns of Lafayette, Moraga, and Orinda. It has a quaint downtown, with oak dotted golden hills on the other side of the train. I sometimes go hiking at the reservoirs nearby.

A group of pretty teen girls enter the train. Somewhat more sophisticated than the girls I went to high school with. Maybe their dads are University professors or European diplomats. The closer you get to the City the more sophisticated things become.

I smile awkwardly but the girls pay no attention. Just more stuck up suburban rich girls. Perhaps I will meet a cool Hipster girl in the City who's into Avant Garde Art and saving the planet.

"Next stop Orinda," another ritzy town.

More people get on, including businessmen commuting into the City and a man with an Asian wife and small child. As I look out the window, I can see the golden hills give way to thick eucalyptus and pine groves and the rolling fog coming in from the other side of the Art Deco, Caldecott Tunnel, which separates the privileged suburbs from the masses of color. The train goes underground and quickly reemerges on the other side of the hills where I get a glimpse of the Bay and SF skyline in the distance. After passing another aerial station where hordes of people board, the train heads back underground.

Once the train stops at Downtown Oakland, I notice a group of African American teen guys lurking near me. I always felt bad for African American youth stuck in poverty with no opportunities, constantly being harassed by racist cops. Yet they still manage to have this sense of pride, confidence, and comradery. You have to be strong when you're an oppressed minority, I suppose.

Suddenly the African American guys surround the rich girls while they obliviously stare at their iPhones. I shouldn't suspect the worst. The guys start chatting them up, but the girls ignore them continuing to text.

One of the guys taunts them, "Yo, don't you like brothas?"

One of the girls awkwardly responds "Yeah."

His friend says "why don't you join us? We throwin a party tonight."

The girl says, "I'm sorry but I have a curfew."

The guys laugh. One says, "You afraid of some niggaz?"

The other guy asks, "you racist ho?"

The girl says apologetically "No, of course not."

"Then why don't you give us yo numbers," he responds.

The girls reluctantly exchange contacts as the African American guys burst out laughing, high fiving each other, as if to say "we got them bitches."

This is like the worst of racist stereotypes. But these guys are outliers. Most African Americans are outstanding citizens. An older Asian man next to me shrugs "look like those girls are in for trouble. Parents should teach better. Grandparents cry. Not allow."

He should know better himself being a marginalized person of color. Looking over, I see the African American guys all have their arms around the girls who look a bit uncomfortable. I was always too anxious to talk to girls of that caliber but these blacks are not only low-inhibition but have the audacity to manipulate them and treat them like objects.

I wonder if they are actually going to their party. What if they end up dating and having sex? I deserve a girl like that not those nig......

What did I almost think? The single most reprehensible word in the English vocabulary. A word single handedly responsible for slavery, lynchings, and Jim Crow.

I can't let my petty jealousies get to me. I guess as hard as I try all White people are racist deep down. That's a scar I just have to live with.

I feel sick to my stomach. The train rattling back and forth, the thought of those beautiful girls with those guys, and the shame of having horrific bigoted thoughts. I look back and see the girls nervously giggling with the African American guys.

Just as I'm about to vomit the train reaches my destination, the Embarcadero Center. Try not to dwell on those negative thoughts. You're in the City now. After breathing in the stale air from the tunnel, I take in a breath of fresh Bay air and my nausea subsides. I decide to explore the Embarcadero Center to take photos for my blog. I have not been there since I was a kid, but I rediscovered the Embarcadero Center from one of the urbanist blogs I follow.

I learned about how the architect who designed it, John C. Portman, was notable for his concept of interior urbanism, and that he was unique in that he was both an architect and developer, and thus could implement his own aesthetic visions.

Anyhow, this place is amazing. Like a cool Retro Futuristic city. It was built in the 70s but it's far more futuristic than any current project. There are skybridges connecting the blocks so there's no need to cross at ground level. A model for a self-contained city, which urbanists call an arcology. And the aesthetics! The slabs of concrete layered over each other intertwined with landscaping like M.C. Escher implemented into urbanism.

I walk up the spiral stairs which go underneath a concrete tulip sculpture. It has bulb lighting which must be magnificent when lit up at night. This is how people should live. But it's practically deserted except for a few businessmen on their lunch break, and some Asian tourists.

I head over to the Hyatt which was also designed by Portman. The atrium is spectacular, like an inverted pyramid, with external glass elevators, and a magnificent sculpture: a cathedral to the gods of Retro Futurism.

After taking in the intoxicating aesthetic splendor I work up an appetite and look for a place for lunch. I feel guilty for not giving the twenty my mom gave me to the houseless, as I promised myself, but I can't spend the day on an empty stomach.

I stop at a sushi restaurant at the Embarcadero and order a spicy tuna roll, miso soup, and jasmine bubble tea which ends up costing most of what I have. I know I have to stay vegetarian, but spicy tuna is just so scrumptious.

After lunch I head out to further explore the City. The vibrancy of the City and extra Klonopin gives me enough energy to walk all day. Without even using Google Maps, I decide to explore on my own. I end up on Broadway which borders Chinatown and North Beach, which is Little Italy. I just love multi-culturalism. We should live in a multi-cultural Disneyland where you visit one country and time-period after another.

Blackstone sort of does that with his themed resorts and he wants to do that with politics too. But his new version of a multi-culturalism based on that theme park model is just regurgitated Jim Crow with a touch of glitz. Besides, wanting to be stuck permanently in some idealized time and place is just a way to avoid confronting the necessity of social progress towards an equal society. We can't segregate and that applies to urbanism too, I suppose.

Anyhow this place is amazing. Lots of neon signs advertising strip clubs on Broadway. Maybe they could be repurposed into something more progressive like feminist bookstores, but the signs are pretty awesome. Must look magical at night.

I walk through North Beach, past all the iconic Italian restaurants and cafes. I accidently bump into a group of Asian tourists as I take photos like a maniac. It's for my blog of course. Everyone in all of the Bay Area is going to know me as the greatest urbanist photo blogger ever.

Down to the Wharf to check out the Bay. It's often fogged in at this time of year but it's sunny enough to see the crystal clear turquoise water with Alcatraz and Marin in the distance. After admiring the views of the Bay, I head over to Ghirardelli Square which is packed with tourists.

As I walk up the steps, I get anxious walking passed the crowds of strangers, but I took an extra Klonopin today and there's so much magnificent architecture to photograph. The brick façades, the retro light fixtures, the incandescent bulb signage, and the old clock tower. A lot of the fixtures were added on when they renovated the old chocolate factory into a shopping complex. Great fusion of old and new.

Why is this just for tourists? They should design entire towns with this aesthetic. A place where people could actually live and work. I so want to get a spiced Chai Latte at the coffee shop, but I already spent all my money on lunch.

I try to take a photo of the mermaid fountain, but it's packed with tourists blocking the view. I realize that I will have to overcome my phobia of crowds if I want to survive today, especially if I want to take the cable car downtown.

Shit! I'm all out of money. I take another Klonopin and wait in queue to get on the cable car. When the attendant asks for admission, I just look away scrunching my face anxiously. An older woman who appears to be a tourist says "oh…he's mentally challenged. Poor young man. I'll cover his cost."

I say "fank you!" Imitating a mentally challenged person, and flap my hands giggling. I'm the biggest scumbag on earth. I'm going to set things right when I win that photo competition and watch smugly as all those transgendered people of color have a chance at life all because of my aesthetic visions.

I feel uneasy squished up against all the sweaty, plus-sized, tourists from flyover country. I just lean to the side and enjoy the magnificent views of the Bay and City, as the Cable Car goes up the hill, making a squeaky noise.

I get off at Nob Hill and take a detour to check out a few sites of architectural significance. At the top of Nob Hill is a park with a really cool renaissance inspired fountain, with statues of turtles, fishes and aesthetically pleasing males, surrounded by some historic hotels with superb lobbies. There's a really cool Tiki lounge at the Fairmont. Walking in the Tonga Room is like being transported to an otherworldly tropical oasis without even stepping on a plane. I'd love to stay but there's so much to see in one day. Hard keeping a mental list of where to go next. I keep repeating the order over and over in my head. I know! Before I head over to Union Square, I'll check out Crocker Galleria.

I look up and admire the retro clock. Like something out of a rail station or 19th Century galleria in Europe. Something about 80's post-modernism that pays homage to the grand aesthetics of the past. A block over is this beautiful golden Art Deco shell in front of the lobby of the Shell Building. Must have been the headquarters for Shell Oil at some point. There was a time when capitalism was actually compatible with aesthetics. A vision for the future rather than just maintaining the current order, or managing decline. Maintaining the current order is the aesthetic of neoliberalism, which is the norm for most newer tech campuses and shopping complexes. No sense of optimism for a greater future.

I remember an interview with Blackstone at the grand opening of his hotel. He said something about San Francisco, and the politics of its aesthetics. Something about the aesthetics of retro-modernism—future oriented yet inspired by aristocratic ideals from the past—triumphing over the decay of late capitalism. Something about how the essence of neoliberalism is that it conceals power.

Roger Blackstone made his fortune in real estate and has just opened the Blackstone Plaza Hotel in South of Market. He has taken on other ventures such as investing in genetic engineering, cryptocurrency, robotics, his own hybrid luxury auto brand (which has an 80's retro aesthetic), and a privately funded highspeed rail that would connect LA to SF and eventually to Seattle and Vegas. Now he's running for president and has developed quite a fascist reputation.

At first I was intrigued by his ideas for a basic income, debt-free banking, legalization of psychedelic drugs, non-intervention, funding for the arts, urban renewal, and alternative energy. But then things got ugly and his supporters started demonizing people of color and he has gone outright fascist, proposing eugenic policies such as re-engineering the human genome and restricting immigration to only the most attractive women, which I assume will mostly be White and blonde. I must stay away from the Blackstone at all costs.

Heading towards Union Square I feel like I'm in the heart of civilization. Taking in the energy of urban life, I observe the Art Deco and Beaux-Arts architecture, high-end department stores like Neiman-Marcus, cool 70's retro towers, some vintage neon signs, and crowds of people. I just can't stop taking photos, of every single angle, every sign, every building. I accidently take a photo of a woman's cleavage. "What the fuck pervert!"

I feel like a real dirtbag but appreciating great architecture trumps everything. After I've photographed every single square inch of the area, I check the time and realize it's getting late. I look up at the Sir Francis Drake Hotel's neon star and sign for the Starlight Room, but it has yet to be lit up.

Despite being nervous about taking BART home at night I want to see the neon signs in the area lit up before I head back. I can even get a glimpse of the Blackstone from Union Square. Don't even think about it, Max.

There's a group of men of color protesting on Union Square chanting "Black Tongues Matter!" One angry African American man shouts on his megaphone "rich white teen bitches from the suburbs be lurrin in our yoof, and usin em like dildos. Keep yo tongue out dem White bitches."

The other man grabs the megaphone "they think their most nastiest parts be higher than the humanity represented by the Black man's face." They all continue chanting "Black Tongues Matter!"

That's odd. I thought interracial romance was a great way to ease inequality. We shall all come together as one. Perhaps if one of those girls let me go down on them, I would feel more at ease about my own White privilege. Curious, I take another Klonopin and approach the men.

After noticing me looking them over, one of the African American men shouts "what you want White boy?"

I say, "shouldn't we support interracial relationships so we can all come together as one?"

He shouts on his megaphone "what you be talkin about? They don't want our dicks. Ever since that crazy ass cracker killed all dem people, these rich White teen bitches started organizen ass n' pussy licken parties."

I thought that was just some urban legend I read about on those incel sites.

I ask "isn't that good for gender and income equality? Teach men to respect the female orgasm and encourage the rich to let the less fortunate into their bedrooms?"

The man yells: "then why the hell don't they get some White boy to do that sheeit? They go and blow all dem White boys and then lure a brotha in. Tie em up, and make em lick all dem asses n' pussies in a box so they don't even have to look at the Black man's face!"

His friend adds "they want to sterilize the Black man. Dats why dem White folks ain't reproducing. White boys be sterile from eaten pussy. They want to sterilize us too. Brothas, don't be eaten dat nasty ass sheeit!"

Perhaps that's what happened with the girls on the BART. I need to become a journalist and expose this injustice to the world. They must stop the exploitation of men of color and instead use those racist incels.

He hands me some pamphlet for their African American Men's Rights organization that says feminism is White Supremacy, promoting eugenics with abortion and an end game of affluent White women enslaving all surviving men of color. Probably some conspiracy to divide and conquer. Turn women against people of color instead of united against the White Patriarchy.

These aren't real feminists. Just stuck up rich girls exploiting a good cause to abuse those who are less fortunate.

I start walking a few blocks west. The area starts to get sketchy and the concentration of houseless people increases just like the number of underprivileged keeps increasing in our society. Blackstone says that we can better provide social services if we reduce the size of the underclass. But we're all born equal. It's just that capitalism denies many a chance at life.

Anyhow, I'm fascinated by the urban grittiness and notice some older vintage neon signs which I quickly snap photos of keeping an eye out for thieves. I see a sign and realize that this is the Tenderloin which my parents have always warned me to avoid but it's much more urban than your typical ghetto.

The further I walk the sketchier things become. I should really head back right after I get a photo of that hotel blade sign. But wait. Right in front of my very eyes is a transgendered houseless person of color, presenting me with the opportunity to provide assistance. I reach into my wallet but all I have is some change. Then I hand her...... I mean them my change. Ze gives me a look of disappointment.

I walk off in shame. One chance to do something unselfish and I blew it. Should have just brought some cheap vegan snacks. Feeling guilty, walking among the downtrodden people of color, I decide to head down to Market Street but there's still a lot of houseless people of color. If I can't be of service, then I'm not worthy to be in their presence.

Panicking, thinking of where to escape to be with my own kind, I look up and there it is. Right up in front of me is the Blackstone Plaza Hotel Tower. A monument to White Privilege towering at up to 60 stories of black glass and gilding over these poor souls. Don't look at it Max. I notice the reflection of animated neon on a glass storefront. Looks like the animated neon of the tower was just turned on.

Inspecting the tower, I notice there are exterior glass elevators, an Art Deco inspired animated gold neon shell on the crown, and on the side the Blackstone Crest glistening like a neon jewel. Brilliant! I have to check it out. Don't let grand aesthetic visions win you over to fascism! Do aesthetics really transcend morality?

Perhaps that's why Blackstone has managed to con a lot of people who wouldn't otherwise support the Right into supporting him. And to make matters worse all his visions are from my dreams. If he gets elected, I'm the one to blame for having those horrible visions that exclude those who don't fit into a certain aesthetic mold.

Everything Blackstone does has some bizarre connection and his new hotel was designed by the famed architect Saul Metzenbaum, protégé of John C. Portman, and ironically, grandfather of the notorious Connecticut killer, Noam. It must have a magnificent atrium like the rest of Metzenbaum's work.

I take in a deep breath and pass through the sliding glass doors. As I anticipated the atrium is massive with black marble, gilding, an Art Deco shell sculpture fountain, and external glass elevators with bulb lighting attached. I can definitely see the influence of Portman.

I really want to get on one of those elevators. Interior with views of the atrium or exterior with views of the City and Bay? There's a sign that reads "Hotel Patrons Only" but after all I have done today, I am already a transgressor against all rules of basic decency so it's too late to turn back now.

I quickly sneak past the sign and onto the elevator. This elevator will take me away to that dream world from my visions where I can just enjoy the aesthetics without stressing about being a righteous person. I can already feel the fascism consume me. Just relax and enjoy the view of the City and Bay. As the glass elevator ascends upwards, I can see the glistening skyline of the City and Bay at sunset. I can even make out the golden highlights of the sunset on Mount Diablo in the distance.

Wouldn't this be a nice place to share a romantic moment with a girl. Like one of those girls from the BART earlier. There's nothing more romantic than an external glass elevator. I really should have gone for it and asked one of them out on a date. They're probably getting licked out by those African American guys right now. They should have just used me instead. My tongue deserves to be sullied with their filth for any insensitive thoughts I may have had.

Nah, just some crazy rumor started by the incels. Cute innocent girls like that would never do something that debased. But isn't that the very essence of capitalism? Anonymously being unaware of your exploitation of others? Those very same girls eat meat from factory farming and use iPhones made in sweatshops by children of color who they never even have to look at. Just like they don't have to look at the faces of the men of color pleasuring them down below.

Some soft calypso synthwave music starts playing. Ah, this music is very romantic. I wonder if it was created by some great Afro-Trinidadian musician. Or is this just the kind of music White Yuppies listened to in the 80's when they vacationed at exclusive resorts in the Caribbean and had people of color wait on them. Cultural Appropriation. The world that Blackstone wants to recreate.

Stop thinking about politics. Just enjoy the view. You don't need a girlfriend right now. Architecture is your one true love. Beauty exists in all shapes and forms, not just girls. I head back to the lobby, where beside the Art Deco shell fountain is that girl from my dreams. I double check. No, it's just a cute Japanese girl in a blonde wig who has some sleazy old businessman hitting on her.

I should go see if the neon signs are lit up around Union Square, but looking at the time, I realize it's getting late. I head over to the Powell BART Station off Market St. It feels like walking around an underground city. There's a tunnel connecting the station to the SF Shopping Centre and another under construction, that in the future will connect it to the new central subway line. There's an advertisement for an under-construction underground shopping arcade that will connect the Blackstone to the BART station and new Muni line. Built by Blackstone of course. Can't wait till it's completed. With no money left, I just sneak through the turnstile. I look at the schedule and the next train will arrive any minute.

I take a brief moment of contemplation. I came to the City to seek enlightenment, take photos of grand aesthetic visions, but something profoundly changed me today after setting foot in the Blackstone. I just can't explain it.

When I get on the train I look around and see groups of young African American men. Some look angry while others joke around with each other. I have just enough benzos in my system that I can look at them naturally without either making direct eye contact, flinching, or having to look away.

After the train passes Oakland, the men all get off and the train is practically deserted. Feels eerie being all alone but you will make it home safe. I look out, noticing the flashing red lights of the station's signage and then a quick glimpse of the animated neon from the Art Deco Orinda Theatre. I got to see my neon sign to end this great day. It's even near my home. I should come back soon to take photos.

After getting off the train, I notice a White Escalade driving

around the parking lot and a helicopter hovering over me.

They must have been surveilling me all day. Luckily my

mom's there in the parking lot to pick me up.

I totally forgot about the presidential debate. After visiting the

Blackstone I kind of want to hear what he has to say. I look

up a clip of the debate which was hosted in Sacramento on

YouTube once I get home. The moderators asks: "what will

you do to address income inequality, including the

disenfranchisement of people of color here in the state of

California?"

Democratic California Senator Dave Cohen-Rodriguez says

"people of color are an integral part of our nation's, and this

great state's, economy. They pick our fruit and run our tech

companies. We need to enforce diversity quotas to ensure that

corporations nationwide reflect the diversity of the world. I

co-sponsored a bill in the Senate that would increase legal

immigration to 3 million a year and mandate that our

workforce reflect the global demographic. My detractors in

my own party have criticized me for voting for Republican corporate tax cuts but once our workforce resembles that of the world, we will have a capitalism that is woke and no longer in need of state regulation."

Republican Governor of Oklahoma, Wilbur Rex Jackson III says "the lunatic environmental lobby in California is driving out the middle class. We need to open federal and state lands to logging and fracking, creating millions of new jobs. Open up land so everyone can enjoy the American dream of owning a home and I would sign Cohen-Rodriguez's bill to open up that dream to people of color from all over the world."

Roger Blackstone who's running unaffiliated and dressed in a purple blazer responds "the fundamental problem in our society is that wealth is concentrated in the hands of a few while the highest population growth is in the underclass, with both trends squeezing out the middle class. If we're going to talk about reforming the distribution of wealth, we must consider the overall demographic structure. To reverse this trend, I would implement a basic income with free healthcare, coinciding with a dramatic cutback in immigration and the elimination of incentives for the underclass to reproduce."

"How would you fund that racist socialist nonsense?" Jackson interrupts.

Blackstone adds "by automating bureaucracy, for one thing, but let me continue. As for the wealthy I propose a financial transaction tax and a tax increase on the top brackets, offset by childcare tax credits for the middle and upper classes to raise their birthrates."

Jackson says "Blackstone's racist proposal to raise the White birthrate is not only an affront to free markets but also the empowerment of women. With paid maternity leave, employers will discriminate against hiring women and shut them out of promotions. And for any woman who does become successful they will only be able to keep the fruits of their labor if they keep popping out kids."

Cohen-Rodriguez says "I'd further extend quotas to insure gender equality in the workforce, especially for women of color. Blackstone's a bigot who would pay underprivileged people of color not to reproduce." Blackstone interjects, "nonsense, I will ensure the profits from automation and privatization are invested back into civilization."

Cohen-Rodriguez responds, "don't buy into Blackstone's phony populism. There are loopholes to protect his own vast fortune. For instance, his tax increase is only directed against the financial and managerial class, exempting innovators and creators, which is just a dog whistle and a way to eliminate the competition. He may raise taxes a bit on some hedge fund but would allow those very same wealthy people that he rants against to deduct that amount just by having some attractive teenage daughter, not to mention he opposes my tax breaks for entrepreneurs of color."

Jackson interrupts "Blackstone wants to take away from our capitalists of color and have White Socialism."

Cohen-Rodriguez adds "it's eugenics plain and simple and does nothing to solve income inequality. As for his immigration policy, People of Color United Against Aesthetic Fascism's study found that 70% of Blackstone visa recipients would be White."

The moderator says: "we will get to immigration shortly but how will you address the affordable housing crisis in California?"

Blackstone responds "restrictions on new housing and high levels of immigration have driven up the cost of housing here in California and both of my opponents' immigration policies would exacerbate that trend. I propose tax incentives and zoning reforms to increase density in urban areas, and retrofit suburbia into walkable communities, while mandating high aesthetic standards."

Jackson interrupts, "This is outright Socialism!" Blackstone responds "increasing the housing supply lowers the cost. You claim to be a capitalist but don't understand the basic principles of supply and demand. Jackson is bought off by big oil and his agenda would ruin this state's ecosystem and beauty which made it desirable in the first place."

Cohen-Rodriguez interjects "Blackstone doesn't care about the environment any more than he cares about affordable housing. I actually have a plan to reform zoning nationally, to ensure a diverse and inclusive future, but if you look closely at Blackstone's zoning proposals you'll see no mention of affordable housing. He just wants to build more luxury developments to enrich his own vast real estate fortune and fulfill some perverse eugenic end," Jackson interjects. "I just want people of color to be able to own single family homes. Is that too much to ask?" Just as the moderator is about to ask about the Blackstone Visas, there's a power outage due to gusty dry winds, causing my internet to go down. I was going to support Cohen-Rodriguez to show solidarity with people of color but are his proposals really the best for the environment? Not to mention he's backed by all the big corporations and banks with the campaign slogan of "Woke Capital." Maybe I'll just vote Green.

Chapter 5: The Aesthetic Revolution

The next day is scorching hot. Feels like 100 degrees out.

I step outside with my morning coffee. The warm dry air intensifies the scent of freshly cut grass, eucalyptus, pine, and various flower blossoms.

When I head back inside to get some air conditioning, Stacey says "Mom, my friends invited me to a pool party at the country club."

"Oh, great Stacey, have a great time."

I really resent Stacey for hanging out with the rich popular crowd. Think about all the hot girls at that pool party. I should sneak in.

Mom says "your dad's out golfing with his buddies. I'm going to the pool with your aunt and cousin. You're welcome to join us."

It's the public pool and I feel like such a loser going there with my family but it's better than staying home alone and I so desperately want to get in some nice refreshing water to cool off.

On the way to the pool we pass by my old high school and there's a massive protest. On one side is a large group of protesters, mostly White progressives, and people of color with signs such as "integrate now!" And on the other side, surrounded by a police barricade are some young men wearing purple Blackstone baseball caps, preppy pastel polos, and 80s style sunglasses. Next to them are a group of respectable looking upper middle-class counter protesters including some with Blackstone for President signs who start to walk away, not wanting to be associated with the lunatics.

My mom says "they're integrating Max's old school by bringing in underprivileged kids from outside the district. We have an ageing population in our community and have the extra space to help the less fortunate."

My aunt mentions that "there are some bigots affiliated with Blackstone called the Aesthetic Revolution. Those creeps have been taking photos of high school students off social media, and ranking high schools on the aesthetics of the student body. Blackstone's for eugenic tax breaks for the rich and his basic income would not apply to underprivileged children, just adults. He would probably base funding for education on the physical appearance of the student body. This all started when Blackstone started talking about reversing declining White birthrates. As if the planet is not overpopulated as it is. Basically, his supporters are a bunch of unemployed perverts who want to leer at high school cheerleaders and feel entitled to government handouts for themselves but not for the most needy."

"Sad," my mom replies.

I remember overhearing some of the hot popular girls in my school saying their dads were going to transfer them to private school due to the proposed changes. It doesn't matter. We have to stand up for the less fortunate and I don't want to end up like one of those unemployed losers in the Aesthetic Revolution who are being promoted on the incel forums. So what if Blackstone will open up sex robot brothels and give incels state funded vouchers to use them, further enriching himself. They are delusional to think that his tax credits for some rich family to have an extra teen daughter will get them a date.

When we get to the public swimming pool, I notice it's crowded as you would expect on a hot summer day. I get uneasy about being in crowds, a sense of being alone in a sea of strangers.

I step in the pool. The water's refreshingly cool but has a sticky feeling to it, as if a bunch of people bathed in it and I'm soaking in their filth.

Noisy little brats keep bumping into me and splashing water. I wish I could just tell them to screw off. I close my eyes and try to imagine I'm in a better place.

Some brat just kicked into me. There's no fucking oasis. You live in a delusional fantasyland. Most of the people swimming here are older people and people of color who come down from disadvantaged communities further north to use the local pool. Just nothing but brown and wrinkled skin.

I remember from past summers there actually being some upper middle-class teens at the pool. But all these social changes, the growing inequality etc., have finally made their way to the local swimming pool, a once great American institution. I just want to handpick all the hottest girls and pack them in like sardines until I suffocate on their perfect smooth skin.

Think about all those brats who get to swim at the country club today. They all get to swim in their private pools and go to their exclusive swim clubs. The injustices of our pool system!

I think about my White Privilege. Yes, I was raised upper middle class but here I am swimming with the proletariat, many of whom probably work tending to the mansions, swimming pools, and country clubs of those very same rich girls I'm denied the honor of watching bathe.

I know I sound like an envious douche right now who tries to politicize and rationalize my proclivities. That's why Blackstone is brilliant.

I still think he's a creep but how would his politics of aesthetics restructure the injustices of our swimming pool system? For starters he would create incentives to increase the number of hot girls. I know that sounds horrible and like a Nazi, but damn I just want to drown to death in pussy right now. And I've seen the proposals for his projects on urbanist blogs where there would be large lake-like communal pools with lots of teens swimming in skimpy bikinis and speedos. And he even has a Pool Act that would invest in and mandate zoning for communal swimming facilities designed by Blackstone's real estate firm. He would also raise taxes on private swimming pools which I suppose is ecologically sound but I think all that it would do is push all those privileged teens into the communal pools so his perverted fans can leer at them. Are my morals sinking that low that I would support a fascist just so I can ogle hot girls?

The Lifeguard blows his whistle and the allocated time for swimming is up. I head over to the men's locker-room while my mom, aunt, and young cousin head over to the women's locker-room.

Once I get to the locker-room to change, I notice there's a group of handsome blonde guys a few years younger than me putting down their backpacks on the bench. My anxiety levels rise.

I don't recognize them from my school. I wonder if they're coming in for swim team or water polo practice. They must be from some exclusive prep school, like Chadsworth Alamo. I wonder why they're using this shitty public pool. I always felt nervous about being nude around other guys but luckily for me most guys at my school didn't shower except for this one fat nerd. My biggest fear was not so much being around naked guys but that I might accidently stare at them. To make matters worse they are younger than me yet of much higher social standing.

Blackstone's platform for education proposes making communal showers mandatory in school and incorporates high school pools and gyms into his urban developments to foster social cohesion. Great way to win the creepy gym coach vote.

I quickly begin to change, trying not to make eye contact but can't help overhearing them boast about girls and parties. I wonder if they're already sexually active? Get over your high school trauma. You don't want to end up like that Noam creep.

Suddenly I turn around. An obsessive-compulsive urge, accidently catching a glance from behind as they're turned away from me, changing. A brief glimpse of smooth toned ass. I close my eyes and take a deep breath in. I shouldn't have to feel this anxious. Excluded from the male bonding that comes so naturally to them.

I learned online that all stratas of Roman Society, which was outright fascist, bathed together nude. Even the slaves were brought to tend to their masters. But these brats wouldn't even grant me that honor. Lower than a slave in their eyes. Not worthy to even make eye contact with them. But I can assure you that I'm not of that persuasion. Not that there's anything wrong with that.

I was in the LGBTQ club in high school to lend my moral support to the cause. But none of those LGBTQ students were aesthetically pleasing. Social rejects just like me. But this has nothing to do with that. It's just my OCD.

As they're changing into their speedos, I briefly look over at them again. Flinching out of fear that I may have seen something I'm not supposed to. I just stare at the puddle on the floor to avoid any risk of making eye contact again. I'll give them another minute to make sure they're done changing.

They all have their Speedos on now but one of them gives me a dirty look. Did they suspect me of trying to catch a glimpse?

Oh, great what if they call the cops on me. And the cops arrest me and throw me in jail with a bunch of gang bangers. I've heard how they treat sex offenders in jail. Especially a skinny White boy like me.

There are certainly no aesthetically pleasing males in a jail shower. Maybe if everyone was aesthetically pleasing, we wouldn't need fascist institutions like Jail where the privileged use the thugs as mercenaries to torment those who challenge their bullshit mores.

I quickly put on my clothes and rush out. I wait outside for my mom, my clothes still soaking wet from not being able to properly dry off. Luckily my mom is ready, and I get in the car.

"Mom, hurry! Drive!" I shout.

"What's wrong Max?" She says

"Ah. I'm just feeling a bit, ill," I respond.

She says, "do you want me to pull over?"

"No, I'll be fine. Let's just go home," I respond.

Chapter 6: The League of Extraordinary Perverts

When I get home, I head to my room and start looking at LGBTQ images online to double check to see if I have any groinal responses. I mean I'm not LGBTQ. I don't think so. Just because you haven't lived up to toxic notions of masculinity doesn't mean you want to pleasure a man.

I take another breath in and start masturbating. I don't feel anything. But these are just some crass images of bears in leather from the Folsom Street Fair, old hairy fat dudes pissing on each other. Gross. Even if I was LGBTQ, I think I could do better.

I remember when I was in the City, I saw a poster that read "Gays for Blackstone, Homonationalism Now." Instead of the usual vulgar imagery that is typical in the LGBTQ community it depicts young athletic blonde guys. Much like the ones I saw in the locker-room.

I get on my computer and look up the website "Gays for Blackstone." It depicts a lakeside surrounded by pines at Blackstone's Alpine Chalet themed resort in Tahoe where young blonde guys swim in speedos while gay men LARP as 18th Century aristocrats, surveilling the view with their monocles.

The caption reads "the homosexual is the natural aristocrat," and goes on about how Blackstone's "Tomorrow's Twinks" initiative of natalist tax breaks for the upper class will breed more aesthetically pleasing males. There's also commentary on how LGBTQ people were the cultural and artistic elite throughout history with quotes from Oscar Wilde.

Blackstone has found a way to unite the perverts on the left and right through the power of aesthetics. Co-opt the artistic LGBTQ community in the City who strive for a Queer culture that recognizes their role as the "natural" cultured elite of this new Athens. Then there's the rich racist perverts who move to exclusive suburbs to get away from people of color, only so they can ogle blonde cheerleaders and jocks in speedos. We mustn't allow our perversions to influence political discourse, especially if it leads to disenfranchising those who don't fit into a narrow concept of what's sexually desirable.

I click on the link for Jews for Blackstone and I see Blackstone at his penthouse on top of the Blackstone Plaza in SF hosting an event for some Jewish charity. The event is a fundraiser to help the victims of the massacre at Chadsworth Academy in Greenwich, Connecticut. That isn't ethically right, and in bad taste considering the killer hero-worshiped Blackstone and a lot of White Supremacists support his campaign.

I start masturbating to all the hot girls attending the school trip from Chadsworth, feeling a little less LGBTQ. Wait. That's the blonde girl from my dreams, the one at the oasis. And Blackstone was in that dream too. I refresh my screen but it says, "video unavailable."

I hear dad yelling. Something about Stacey. She hasn't come home yet and it's past ten, her curfew. I hope she's not with that disgusting guy I saw her talk to at the mall. She never would even talk to me in front of her popular friends. Stacey comes home an hour later and rushes into her room and shuts the door.

Having trouble sleeping thinking about all this stuff.

As I'm headed to the bathroom to take a piss, I hear something.

"I can't believe Sasha. She actually had a guy down there. Yeah like I know."

What is Stacey talking about?

I put my ear closer to her door to eavesdrop.

Stacey says "yeah, that must feel like really good, but I don't know about having some random guy do that."

This can't be what I suspect. That urban legend about rich popular high school girls having oral sex parties where one girl sits down like she's on the toilet and some guy eats her out from inside a box. And Sasha's so fucking hot too. I can't imagine what that would be like for the guy down below. Maybe I should try to apply, but I'm too privileged as they get off on abusing the most vulnerable.

I do some research on the new incel site that was set up after the old one got shut down and they are proposing some concept where incels are used for oral pleasure by rich popular girls. The idea was put forth in Noam's manifesto, but rumor has it the very same popular girls who rejected Noam have co-opted his idea and transformed it into some feminist cause. They're trying to turn the tables against the males whose misogyny led to the massacre, but ironically, are themselves using the idea as a tool of further class oppression.

But is it really punishment to get to do that to a girl way out of your league? Even if they view your face, the house of your senses, the thing you experience the world with, the thing people recognize you by, and your mouth: your highest orifice, the thing which you eat and speak with... even if they view all of it as only worthy of being placed on their lowest parts, their ass and pussy. Where they piss, bleed, and shit from. Sitting upon you like an object, only there to be used as their personal dildo and douche and then disposed of. I know this isn't about equality but I'm able to cum multiple times in a row fantasizing about that scenario.

The next day I spend my time uploading the photos from the City to my blog, "Max's Aesthetic World."

My mom comes in and says "dad's heading to Dublin to visit an old friend. You two could use some father son bonding time."

Dublin is a suburb about 20 minutes south. I hate being alone in the car with my dad with his rightwing racist rants but feel pressured and don't want to disappoint my mom who has done a lot to help me get through this rough year.

As we're driving dad turns on AM News Radio. The newscaster announces,

"Inside Meschel's nefarious Casting Couch: Formerly beloved director Ari Meschel has been accused of sexually harassing actresses on the set of his new teen drama 'Chad Love', a light-hearted parody of the sexual fantasies of Connecticut Killer Noam Metzenbaum. Several of the actresses have alleged that Meschel would disrobe, masturbate in front of them, and then proceed to perform oral sex on them in exchange for roles. The #MeToo movement is demanding his resignation from Meschel Pictures."

My father remarks "Meschel, that filthy Jew bastard." This is a new low even for him. I look at him in disappointment.

He says "look, I have nothing against the Jews. I think Ben Shapiro is fantastic and the Israelis need to bomb the Arabs back to the stone ages. It's the communist Jews who run Hollywood I have a problem with. But once we elect Jackson he will clean up all this filth. Not like that commie Cohen-Rodriguez and that Blackstone. Don't get me started on him. Giving out free money to moochers like candy, and promoting UN Agenda 21 in our very own backyards. Not to mention, he's an even bigger perv than Meschel. If he has his way our neighborhood will be packed with teens fornicating and getting high by the creek.

I say "oh come on. Hollywood is capitalism in its purest form. It treats women as a commodity to exploit rather than as human beings. And Jackson will just cut taxes on those same Hollywood types he bashes to rally up his base."

He turns up the volume to cut me off. The radio announces "Breaking News. The Aesthetic Revolution has struck again. An assault occurred against a local lawyer at his residence in Alamo. The suspects also shouted racial and body-shaming epithets at his housekeeper and spray painted the logo of the Aesthetic Revolution on his property. The lawyer whose name is not being disclosed is best known for suing to block Roger Blackstone's Oasis Resort development in Alamo. Suspects are in custody on charges of vandalism, assault, elder abuse, and ethnic intimidation."

The reporter continues "the Aesthetic Revolution's propaganda mirrors Blackstone's campaign proposal for urban renewal and eugenic policies of childcare tax credits for wealthy families while paying the less fortunate not to reproduce. Members of the Aesthetic Revolution have also been harassing students of color transferring to local schools, reminiscent of anti-desegregation violence on grounds that it debases the aesthetics of the student body. Blackstone's campaign proposal calls for an end to school busing, school vouchers for private schools, and his campaign platform on education shows imagery of a student body that is disproportionately White. Federal Authorities are investigating whether the Aesthetic Revolution has ties to the Blackstone campaign."

Dad turns off the radio, "fucking losers need to get out of their mommies' basement, go get a real job, and get laid." He points to the hillsides being carved into to make way for a new subdivision, "this is capitalism at its finest. The American dream! Some day if you work hard you might be able to buy one of these homes." I think about all the greedy White people who work for corporations who buy these McMansions.

We finally arrive at my dad's friend's house in Dublin. He's an older Japanese American man who my dad has known since before I was born. The home is the only aesthetically pleasing house on the block which was remodeled into a Japanese style Mid-Century Modern aesthetic with a Japanese garden, koi pond, and collection of Bonsai trees.

My dad and his friend get into a debate about Blackstone which I find amusing. My dad goes on about how Blackstone's a socialist and eco-fascist and his friend talks about how Blackstone has invested in his new robotics company, that he's good for innovation, and even gave him a loan through his company to retrofit his home to be more aesthetically pleasing.

After we leave the house we get stuck in rush-hour traffic from all the new subdivisions and their inhabitants heading home from work. Dad says pointing at the cars, "all the Pajeets trying to steal my job."

I look around and see mostly immigrants of color. Are these people any better than the White Capitalist Pigs? Capitalism sees no race. It's all about money. DCR, Dave Cohen-Rodriguez, is wrong when he says that capitalists of color are more progressive but you can't end up a fascist Blackstone supporter. But Blackstone isn't just another conservative. He wouldn't develop something this atrocious. His projects are actually walkable and respect their natural surroundings. But a lot of fascists have historically adopted some progressive views to mask their bigotry.

Maybe my dad is right to be angry but why is he voting for Jackson who wants to increase foreign tech visas and deregulate the Tech Industry? Blackstone would nationalize Big Tech as a utility, and use the revenue generated from automation for greater things. I also like Blackstone's proposal to turn tech campuses into self-contained eco-cities.

The next few days I spend lounging around the house waiting for school to start. My mom is spending the day with her cousin who's visiting from Wisconsin, my sister is staying at her friend's mansion, and my dad is golfing with his friends, so I have the house to myself. But I have too much anxiety to head out since I'm low on Klonopin with nothing to calm my nerves except some Bud Lights my dad left in the fridge.

I spend most of my time watching porn and videos of Roger Blackstone. Sometimes simultaneously. Cumming to every articulation and nuance of his political philosophy and aesthetic imagery. I hear giggling coming from next door. I step outside, breath in the warm dry air, and peek through the bushes to see what's going on next door.

I look over through the bushes and see the blonde neighbor girl, Chloe, with her Asian friend whom I also recognize from school. Both in lacy bath robes. I quickly guzzle down two beers to build up some courage and head back outside. I feel like such a creep, but I can't help myself.

The two girls, giggling, seem to be taking shots. Do their parents even know they're drinking? Girls do crazy stuff when they're drunk. Chloe starts to disrobe. Overwhelmed by the thought of seeing them nude.

Nah, but it's a really skimpy bikini with a shell bikini top. The two girls start giggling again. I should really ask to join them and not watch as a creep from the sidelines. The Asian girl then takes off her robe. The two girls standing there in their designer bikinis. Then Chloe takes some water from the pool and splashes it on her friend.

I've always fantasized about swimming with her. What a romantic experience it would be to swim with two beautiful girls and not spend another summer alone, daydreaming about what I'm missing out on. Seize life and take action for once or end up old and alone, forever haunted by the young love you never had. Just seeing the two girls overwhelms me with romantic and lustful feelings. I could never imagine actually getting the chance to hang out with them. I doubt she even knows I exist. Would they even hangout with me if I asked?

Suddenly the two girls jump in the pool. Should I shout out: "may I come over and join you?"

Nah, I'll just hide out here in the bushes but I'd better be cautious not to let them see me.

After being titillated by watching them splash water on each other, Chloe jumps up on an inflatable flamingo and starts twerking. Her ass up in the air with her thong bikini stuffed in her crack. Her perfect plump smooth ass appears completely exposed.

I intensely zoom-in, analyzing all of the details; from the light peach fuzz and subtle rash on her cheeks, to the pale tan lines around her crack, and for a brief moment I can visualize what it would be like for the guys used by the rich girls at those parties. I wonder if she's ever attended one? Perhaps if I sneak in they will use me at one of those parties as punishment for being a peeping tom.

Nervously shaking, envisioning the scenario, I trip, falling into the bush making a noise. The girls in the pool freeze and I panic. Suddenly they turn around and see me there peeking through the bushes. Screeching "eeeeeeeeeeeeeeeek!"

Then they quickly get out of the pool, cover themselves in their towels, and run inside. I run inside too panicking. All worst-case scenarios running through my head. I just hide out in my room anxiously sipping another beer. I could really use a Klonopin right now, but they don't always mix well with alcohol.

About a half an hour later I hear a police siren outside and a chopper hovering above our house. Then I hear knocking on the door.

"Police! Open up!"

I'm petrified. Making matters worse, I'm starting to really feel the Klonopin withdrawal.

"Police! Open up. Now!

I peek out the window through the curtains. Oh shit. My parent's car is in the driveway and I hear my dad yelling "what the fuck is going on here?"

The door opens and I see my mom in tears, my dad with an angry expression, as two stern police officers enter. I'm petrified of being arrested. And forget about ever having a career as a journalist.

To my relief the Police Officer turns to my parents and says, "under these circumstances we can't make an arrest but I'd advise you keep a close eye on your son."

My father responds "will do. Thank you for your service."

The officers don't respond and head off. My mom runs into their room to cry.

My dad grabs me by the collar. I've never seen him this angry before.

He shouts "what the fuck were you thinking? You wouldn't last one hour in jail!"

I start sobbing. My father punches me on my shoulder.

"Don't cry like a little bitch. You're a man now. Take responsibility for your actions and try to find a woman your own age."

In tears, I let out my most vulnerable secret.

"Look dad. I never had a girlfriend in high school. I want to know what young love is like before it's too late."

Dad warns me in a calm but stern voice, "if you ever say that again you're out on the streets."

He then heads off to his room where I can overhear him trying to comfort my crying mom.

I head to my room in tears. I've never felt this humiliated in my entire life. I know I made a mistake but I deserve a special someone. The perfect teen romance before I move on to the drudgery that is adult life. Take the age pill and accept, as the incels lament. That's a privilege reserved only for Chad. I peek out the window and see the White Escalade parked out across the street as the chopper still hovers above our house.

The next morning there's cold silence at the breakfast table. Mom pours me coffee and orange juice but remains silent. Luckily Stacey's not here to ridicule me.

After an hour of silence, dad informs me, "you messed up big time son. You really disappointed me. You're grounded for a week until your summer session starts."

I protest "grounded? But I'm an adult."

Dad responds "as long as you live under my roof, you're under my rules. That means no internet or leaving the house, not even going outside in the backyard.

Chapter 7: My Asian Girlfriend

The next week I spend endless hours lying in bed, contemplating the purpose of my existence. I had big dreams in high school, of being on the path to becoming a well-respected journalist. Enjoying the college experience and meeting the girl of my dreams who I can impress by making the world a better place. But in reality what have I accomplished?

Maybe I am a loser and none of my political ideals or urbanist blogging and photo journals mean jack shit. Just silly hobbies. The last few days are more bearable since my mom has refilled my Klonopin at the pharmacy.

As soon as I take my pills I'm out of my depressed anxious state and just chill, trying to regain a sense of optimism and make the best of my situation.

I start my first day at City College, excited about all the intellectually stimulating classes I signed up for. I look around and notice that the City College is a lot more diverse than my high school which was predominantly White and fairly affluent. Perhaps I will be more accepted in a more diverse and inclusive environment?

Most of these students must be from lower income communities further north. All the popular girls with wealthy parents from my high school must have gone off to exclusive universities back East or to party schools. As much as I resented them, I feel left behind. Even though I was rejected I kind of miss just being in their presence.

I'm not a standardcel like that killer Noam who coped with his inadequacies and struggles to live up to his White Privilege with delusions of Aristocracy and a racist preference of only being attracted to blonde, White girls. I remember some celebrity getting heat for saying something like my heart loves everyone, but my dick's racist. But sexual racism is just as bad as any other form of bigotry.

Let me try to keep count of all the girls of color I was attracted to. There were quite a few actually. But they were still all from relatively privileged backgrounds and all went on to great universities. Would Blackstone's programs spread beauty across all class lines rather than just a luxury reserved for the elites, a kind of aesthetic Marxism?

Overcome with shame, I start starring at the asses of the girls of color and envision they're using me at those parties. I shouldn't be objectifying them like that. It's bad enough I'm walking around with a massive hardon and I'm almost late to my first class which is on Economic Theory.

In class I start to daydream about the girl from the oasis as the professor goes on and on about economics. Then I hear the name Blackstone which grabs my attention. The Professor explains this concept of Positional Goods which are goods that are in limited supply due to their value relative to others. He strongly dislikes Blackstone, but admits that he has unlocked the key of how to win people over by addressing their untapped desire for positional goods.

This really hits me because I have always had my basic needs of food, shelter, and healthcare taken care of, but the things that I have deep, unmet desires for are all positional: primarily access to people, locations, and things of aesthetic value. The professor goes on that the fundamentals of Blackstone's platform are to increase the supply of positional goods. Appealing to the middle class who strive to become wealthy by providing this image of a bourgeoise utopia where everyone is rich because everyone and everything is aesthetically pleasing.

The Professor explains that Blackstone would increase the supply of luxury housing for the petite bourgeoise, but the catch is it would be developed by his real estate firm, filling his pockets. He adds he would also appeal to the racial anxiety of the White upper-middle-class who view being around "the right kind of White" people as a Positional Good. He'd do this by giving them natalist tax breaks and ending anti-discrimination laws in housing, propagating the bigoted notion that there's competition over a limited number of desirable

people. None of which will do anything to address inequality.
Just bribing the proletariat with a basic income, which he'd
make conditional on eugenic grounds, while nice things are
still only for the rich, just making the size of the upper class
larger. And are his policies even that ecologically sound,
catering to the materialistic desires of the bourgeoise?
Contributing to overpopulation by encouraging the privileged
to breed even more offspring who will consume more than
their fair share, leaving nothing for people of color.

I need to get over my classist concepts of beauty and
unfulfilled obsessions about failing to live up to my own
White Privilege.

My next class is Environmental Journalism. My two areas of
expertise.

As the teacher calls roll a certain girl catches my attention.

"Lilly Nguyen."

I need to ask her out after class and get over the shame of
never having been on a date. Plus dating a girl of color will

help me feel just a little less shitty about myself. JBW, just be White, as the incels say. And besides she's really cute.

The discussion in our class today is whether the issue of overpopulation is politically sensitive in environmental journalism due to the fact that it could lead to xenophobic sentiment. I don't want to risk offending Lilly but I have nothing else to say that no one has said and want to be bold and prove myself as a great freethinker instead of just following the heard like I did in high school, which got me nowhere.

The Professor calls on me and I anxiously answer.

"We must not simply look at climate change as a global issue but consider the dramatic increase in the ecological footprint of immigrants who move here from the developing world and go on to buy McMansions and SUVs in the suburbs."

The entire class gives me a dirty look and the Professor is looking at me like I fucked up big time.

I look over at Lilly, but she's not upset. She has the look that she respects my courage for standing up for what I believe in. Even if it's not popular. After class I see Lilly in the hallway. I feel anxious but my extra Klonopin gives me a little courage and I'm desperate to find a girlfriend, so I decide to go for it.

"Hi, Lilly"

"Oh, hi," she replies.

I put out my hand for a formal handshake, "My name is Max. Max von Mueller."

Lilly laughs, "I think everyone knows your name by now. You're notorious."

"Oh, am I? I respond."

She says, "but I always liked bad boys," half joking with the awareness I'm the biggest dweeb.

Cutting to the chase I ask, "would you like to hang out some time?"

Lilly giggles awkwardly. I'm terrified of rejection.

To my surprise she says, "sure why not," and we exchange

contacts. I'm going on my very first date. The beginning of a

new life.

Chapter 8: The Art Bro

My next class is broadcasting. I've always wanted to be a TV news anchor, no a journalist. Not just another narcissistic douchebag but actually someone who enlightens the public about all the injustices facing the world.

I look around the class. Lots of over-socialized middlings, students of color, who like their privileged counterparts, strive to make it in corporate media by memorizing all the right talking points. And then there's the douchebags, perhaps the most popular students from low income high schools. Less aesthetically pleasing versions of the popular guys at my high school.

One in particular makes me ill. He has a man bun, appropriating the culture of the great South Asian Warrior Caste. He looks like he purchased his clothes at Urban Outfitters, and has tacky tribal tattoos, gauged earrings, and swarthy ethnically ambiguous looks, not to mention a smug arrogant expression that says I'm a slacker but at least I got laid in high school. He probably grew up in some suburban shithole further north but is like a wannabe version of the Art Bros who have wrecked the entire Hipster scene including some of my favorite art galleries.

I used to be fascinated by the hipster scene but then all these bros and former jocks from the suburbs came into Oakland and the City and ruined it all. Maybe Blackstone's Fashy Hipsters aren't that bad after all. At least they have class.

I also notice that this class has an unusual concentration of pretty girls for the College. One girl in particular stands out, named Natasha. She's a pretty bubble blonde with slightly ethnic features, reminding me of some of the popular girls I went to high school with who tried to look edgy. I shouldn't be fantasizing about other girls when I have a date set up with Lilly but I can't help feeling lust for her. The Professor divides the class up into groups and each student will be assigned roles including newscasters, cameramen, and some low-level production roles. I'm put in a group with Natasha and the Art Bro, Blake which both terrifies and excites me.

Blake suddenly takes over the group and puts his arm around Natasha, "you and me. Stars of the show."

It's time for the group to vote. I'm anxious about getting a low status role.

As I expected Blake and Natasha are the lead news anchors. Even worse I'm assigned the role of production assistant. It sounded prestigious at first but then I found out that my only role will be to move around props, and worst of all bring coffee and sodas to Blake like his servant.

I must prove my status. I quickly take another Klonopin while no one is looking and protest, "I'm the only one here actually dressed for the role. Perfect buttoned light blue dress shirt. You all are dressed like slobs."

I have never confronted other students in my entire life, but I have all this pent up rage left over from high school and this is the first time I felt the confidence to let it all out.

Blake bursts out laughing, spitting his soda all over everyone, "what a dweeb."

Natasha jokes "he's totally going to shoot up the school. I'm like so afraid."

I rush out of class, humiliated, while they continue to mock me. But it doesn't matter. I have a date this weekend. I text Lilly to set up a date for Saturday.

The only problem is I don't have a car and mass transit sucks in this region. I'm too embarrassed to be picked up in front of my house so I arrange to meet her for coffee in Downtown Walnut Creek. The coffee shop has a Hipster aesthetic, all grey and lime green, with high ceilings and small but tall wood tables. I used to find the aesthetic innovative, but it's now become so banal.

While we're sipping our Chai Lattes and making awkward small talk a group of cheerleaders from my old high school walk in giggling. One of them sneers, remembering me staring at them from the bleachers during cheer practice. Even though I have a girlfriend now who is intelligent and respects me I can't help getting stuck on these popular high school girls.

After we're done, we head out for lunch. I suggest Danville because it's on our way to the surprise destination. Lilly wants to take the highway, but I suggest that the side streets are more scenic. I feel a bit emasculated with her driving with me in the passenger seat, but I try to take charge by giving her directions.

I can't help but get distracted by the scenic drive: big mansions, ranches, oak trees, and golden hillsides. This is Alamo, an exclusive residential community where Roger Blackstone has his estate and where his under-construction Oasis Resort will be.

I notice a Waspy looking man driving a vintage 80's Jaguar, with a cute blonde teenage daughter in shotgun, and a Blackstone for President sticker on the bumper. Blackstone's coalition seems to be an eclectic mix including some Old Money types who he's able to woo over with imagery of an all-White utopia. These types mingle with outsiders ranging from social outcasts and Avant Garde artists, Silicon Valley techno-fascists, hipsters for the ironic value, working class

White people in flyover country, those who just want the Blackstone bucks, and environmentalists who want clean energy and ecologically sustainable development. What a coalition.

We pull up for lunch in Downtown Danville, an upscale town with a quaint Old West aesthetic. Probably a real Old West town at some point before it got absorbed into suburbia.

We park at a really cool shopping complex which looks like a mountain lodge. There's a gourmet pizza place where we end up ordering limonatas to drink, a gorgonzola salad, and a margherita pizza to share. Right behind Lilly is a group of good-looking blonde preppy teens, perhaps on dates. Some ageing hippie jokes, "Blackstone's Hitler Youth."

I'm further intrigued, noticing their ritzy Chadsworth Alamo uniforms, and it's as if Blackstone has been using the school for his breeding program.

I try to keep the conversation going with Lilly but can't help getting distracted by them, glancing at them and then trying to keep eye contact with Lilly. I'm worried she can tell I'm obviously distracted but says nothing and tries to keep the awkward small talk going.

As the teens leave, one of the girls notices me staring and lifts up her skirt to expose her lacey panties, mocking me. I briefly catch a glimpse of her panties and notice the phrase on her ass: "your best is only good enough for my worst."

I wonder if that's part of the secret society the incels were talking about?

None of that matters. It's just me and my girlfriend. I look her in the eyes and tell her I'm going to take her to my favorite special place.

She asks "where?"

I respond: "it's a surprise."

Lilly smiles assuring me that the date is still salvageable.

We get in Lilly's car. I look at Google Maps and try to direct her but keep getting distracted by the scenery. Lilly's not the greatest driver so I have to stay focused. With the swerving narrow roads, bicycles in the way, and Lilly driving like a maniac I feel a bit carsick.

I look out at the view. I have not been up this far in a long time.

Lilly complains "this is so scary. We should head back."

I demand, trying to prove my dominance, "no, you have to see the view at the top. It's spectacular."

Lilly gives me an annoyed look, but continues driving. There are some groves of pines on a lookout. I totally forgot how amazing this place is.

We stop briefly at a pine grove where there's an old cabin and campground. The view is already amazing from here but I'm restless to get to the summit. When we get back in the car Lilly starts driving back down the mountain.

"Lilly, you're headed the wrong way," I say.

Lilly thought we had already reached our destination.

Annoyed she pulls onto the shoulder, nearly hitting a cyclist and heads back up.

The road gets even narrower and more winding. How do these cyclists make it without crashing?

Finally there, I get out of the car anticipating the view from the summit. Lilly stays in the car with the air conditioning on at full blast. The air smells and feels amazing; warm, dry gusty winds, with a scent of pine.

Lilly finally gets out of the car and looks around. I turn to her, "this is Mount Diablo. On top of the world."

She doesn't look as excited as I anticipated. I thought she was into nature like I am.

I suggest we head over to the observation tower but she complains "it's sooo hot up here and goes back to the car to get her water bottle.

After she's finished I shout, "Lilly come on."

Lilly says she's going to wait in the air-conditioned car.

I head off to the observation tower on my own. I've dreamt of taking my first date to the summit of Mount Diablo ever since I was a freshman in high school, but she doesn't seem enthusiastic at all.

The observation tower is cool, almost like a medieval watch tower. To the east I can see the vast Central Valley with the Sierras in the distant haze and north out over the Delta. Then I look out to the west. Looking straight down, I can see the rugged ridges and foothills glistening in gold, a tree covered area of suburbia ranging from Danville to my home in Walnut Creek. Beyond there I can see the golden hills with patches of blueish-green woodlands around the Lamorinda area. And in the distance, emerging from the fog, I can see the skyline of the City peak out. The Transamerica Pyramid, Salesforce Tower, and the Blackstone Plaza Hotel, Blackstone's Art Deco tower adding a dynamic to the boxy Skyline.

After I'm done taking pictures for my blog, I head back to the car to check on Lilly. She's inside with a bored expression. I really have to find a way to make this a special moment for us.

I bang on the car door. She comes out and sighs.

I grab her hand and walk over to check out the view from the parking lot. "Isn't this spectacular?" I ask.

Lilly says "oh yeah. It's nice I guess."

I state, "this is nature, the view and all."

Lilly responds "Yeah, I guess. But it's just sooo hot."

My voice changes from wonder to slight annoyance.

"Don't you appreciate nature? I mean we met in an environmental journalism class."

She responds "I do, but I'd rather be in a nice cool Redwood forest or by the Sea. This is like a desert."

Maybe I should have just taken her to Tilden Park or the Redwoods near Oakland. I lean in for a kiss, but Lilly awkwardly backs away.

On the drive down we barely talk. I tell Lilly to drop me off in Downtown Walnut Creek. I lean in for a hug and she responds with a polite yet platonic hug back, giving mixed signals.

I walk home in the heat thinking about whether I had screwed things up with Lilly, but now that I think about it, I was too focused on the spectacular view to pay attention to her concerns. I keep playing over the scenario nonstop in my head over the weekend. I take another pill to calm down the obsessive thoughts.

In the next Environmental Journalism class, I sit down next to Lilly who smiles assuring me everything is fine. The rest of the class gives me cold looks but I don't care. I will use this class to enlighten myself intellectually and spend time with Lilly.

After class I talk to Lilly in the hall and assure her that I will make it up to her and do something really special. Lilly smiles and says jokingly "you better."

She gives me a hug and we both head off.

Next class is Broadcasting. I look over and see the cocky, douchebag, Art Bro flirting with Natasha. At this point it's not really about my lust for Natasha but proving to that Douchebag who's boss here. The only problem is that they already enforced the social hierarchy by assigning me to be their Production Assistant bitch.

As soon as I sit down Blake orders me to go get him a soda from the vending machine.

At first, I try to ignore him but the entire group is staring at me to go do my job. I have to prove that I'm the best damn production assistant there is.

I head over to the Vending Machine to get a Sprite. I quickly run back in and open it, but the soda fizzes up and sprays all over Natasha's cleavage, and worse makes her shirt see through so everyone can see her breasts which I'm now staring directly down at.

Natasha screeches "you fucking loser!"

Blake says smugly "that isn't' cool bro. That's sexual harassment."

Natasha says "he's right. I'm going to report him."

She quickly takes her phone and types out loud: "hastag MeToo."

Am I just as big of a creep as Meschel or worse: the incels?

I come home after a disastrous day and notice there's a for sale sign on our neighbor's property. I wonder if they left because of that incident?

This sounds creepy and all but ever since my freshman year I would ride my bike around the neighborhood. Every year I would check the area to see how many hot girls lived nearby. The girls would graduate and head off to college or their families would move out and be replaced by retirees from the City, or mediocre-looking couples in Tech who likely won't ever reproduce.

Anyhow my own census found a decline by 30% in hot girls over a 4-year period. Maybe this is what Blackstone is talking about when he says that wealth must serve the demographic aesthetic good. I should send him my data. No, you have a girlfriend now who appreciates you for who you are. No more spergouts, creepy stalker shit, and daydreaming about random unattainable girls.

Chapter 9: Heaven is a Place on Earth

Due to the incident with Natasha I decide to avoid school and tell my parents I'm ill. Lilly texts me to see if I'm ok and I tell her that I'm mourning my grandmother's passing. A way to both get sympathy and for her not to think I'm contagious if we do go on another date soon. I tell Lilly that I want to take her to Santa Cruz for the day. She's thrilled.

Since my family is gone for the day I have Lilly pick me up at my home. I tell her that I'm renting a room to avoid the embarrassment of admitting I live with my parents. We head off to our destination. We drive down the 680 towards the Silicon Valley.

Once we reach Fremont we get into a traffic jam, even on a Saturday morning. Do these corporate slaves even get weekends off? Lots of crazy Asian drivers. Maybe Lilly isn't such a bad driver after all. I look at her and smile. I'm starting to fall for her. She might actually be the one.

We drive though the Santa Cruz Mountains. Very beautiful, but a different natural aesthetic than Mount Diablo. I can't decide what I prefer; the oak woodlands and golden hills or the lush Redwoods. Nature is spectacular in all its forms. We stop at the Redwoods at Henry Cowell State Park for a picknick. I picked up Sushi, barbeque kettle chips, and sparkling water from Whole Foods and Lilly brought some homemade Vietnamese Pho. It's a nice sunny day with cool fresh air and I can hear the sounds of the ancient Redwoods creaking along with the rushing water of the stream.

Lilly turns to me and smiles. I'm so happy she appreciates nature. I don't think I can fall in love with a girl who doesn't. As we drive down to Santa Cruz, Lilly is slowly getting adjusted to driving on winding mountain roads. A brief stop in Downtown Santa Cruz, a charming historic college town. Lilly mentions she wants to check out the Boardwalk. It's a location by the sea with lots of pastel colored structures and retro neon, magical even with the crowds of proles coming in from inland areas to escape the summer heat.

Lilly gets a cotton candy for us to share. I see the pink sticky goo on Lilly's lips and so want to kiss her but now is not the time. Lilly suggests we go on the Giant Dipper. I'm petrified of roller coasters, but I have a brave girl, no a brave woman of color, to protect me and hold my hand.

My stomach growls from the cotton candy and anticipation of the ascent up. I hold Lilly's hands tightly. My hands are sweaty, but she doesn't mind. As we slowly ascend up the roller coaster, I get more petrified holding her hand even tighter. I hope my hand isn't sweating too much.

Once we approach the top, I close my eyes. The view must be superb, but I guess I'll miss out on that aspect of the experience. It's over quickly and not as horrifying as I anticipated, but I feel a bit dizzy. I sit down on a bench to rest. Lilly comforts me asking if I'm feeling alright.

I get up and grab Lilly's hand and carry her off into the neon wonderland. I hear some 80's music playing. I pull Lilly over to check out the scene. There's an 80's themed dance club with cool animated neon shapes that dance to the music.

The song "Heaven Is a Place on Earth" by Belinda Carlisle is playing. I remember that song being referenced in Noam's manifesto as he drove his vintage Beamer around Greenwich. The philosophy of Belinda Carlisle is that being in a romantic relationship is the only way to achieve Heaven on Earth. Therefore, being alone in a romantic setting like this would be a personal Hell. Luckily for me I have a girlfriend.

Despite not being religious, I give a quick prayer for all the social outcasts and romantically rejected men in the world, as well as the victims of the few who lash out in violent eroticized rage like Noam did.

Lilly noticing my contemplation grabs my hand and pulls me out onto the dance floor. I'm not the greatest dancer but it doesn't matter. It's just about me sharing this special moment with my girlfriend, transported into a romantic 80's teen movie. Dancing as we hold each other's hands spinning around in circles.

The next song is "Like a Prayer" by Madonna. The song is a beautiful love story about an interracial couple in The South who had to hide their love from racist barbarism. I feel a bit guilty for every time I felt resentment for seeing an African American hit on a pretty White girl and a bit schizophrenic for simultaneously being moved by this song while also appreciating the fascist synthwave that Blackstone's supporters have been making. But everything with an 80's sound or aesthetic can be romantic, and it doesn't matter because I have my own interracial love story. I hum to the lyrics, "I just want my little Asian girlfriend down on her knees, and she will take me there."

The next song is Billy Joel's "This is the Time." It's a slow dance. I hold onto Lilly tightly just wanting to savor this special moment because as the song says "It will not last forever."

Just as I'm enjoying this magical moment, a group of blonde teen girls surround us. No, not just any blondes, but blonde Jewish girls. Like Alicia Silverstone's character in that cheesy 90's film The Crush. And they don't even have guys with them.

I never thought about girls with those specific features until reading about them in Noam's manifesto. And then I kept seeing that blonde Jewish girl in my visions and immediately fell in love with her.

I found it bizarre at first but they have a special mystique. Girls of mixed Jewish and Nordic heritage. Pretty blonde girls but with slightly exotic features. They're more common in LA but there were some girls like that in my high school. I never really thought about them that way until recently.

I have Jewish cousins because my aunt in LA married a Jewish Hollywood Producer who ironically worked with the infamous Ari Meschel. But I doubt he has a Casting Couch. I even inspected every single room in their home for Casting

Couches but all I found was a nice white leather family friendly sofa, totally unsullied by bodily fluids.

Anyhow, last summer my cousin invited me to her Sweet 16 pool party at their mansion in Calabasas, which is a wealthy suburb of LA. There were so many hot blonde Jewish girls in thong bikinis but every single one of them ignored me.

I felt so devastated that I ran into the bathroom to cry and was depressed on the entire car ride home, especially while looking out over the sunset on the Pacific Ocean. This is your chance to finally talk to some. No, your girlfriend is right in front of you.

The next 80's classic is "Valerie" by Steve Winwood.

I grab Lilly's hands for the dance. Dancing as the song lyrics go "Call on me." The animated neon still dancing alongside us.

Those girls are really cute in their short skirts. I need to convince Lilly to buy me some candy and then ask one of the girls to dance before she comes back. But it's too late. Lilly catches me staring at the girls and runs off in tears.

The song "Heavenly Action" by Erasure starts playing as Lilly leaves. My favorite band of all time. This would have been the best song to dance with Lilly to. Transcending to a euphoric state of pure ecstatic love with my "Angel made in Heaven." A moment I would have cherished for the rest of my life. I have to find her and make things right.

I rush down to the beach to look for her. She turns around. Noticing me she starts quickly walking away.

I can still hear the faint melody of Erasure. I follow her but she screams: "I don't want to speak with you!"

This would have been the most romantic magical moment with the sunset, scent of sea air, the sound of seagulls and crashing waves, and neon glistening from the Boardwalk in the background, but I ruined everything.

I try to put my arm around Lilly to comfort her but she cries, "go away. I never want to speak to you again."

She sits down on the sand. Should I try to comfort her? Or just give her some time alone to calm down?

What if she leaves without me and I'm completely stranded, forced to take the Greyhound home with the dregs of society? I just continue to pace up and down the beach keeping an eye on Lilly.

Eventually Lilly gets up. I slowly follow her from a distance to the parking structure. We both get in the car, avoiding eye contact as if we've never met.

To distract from the awkward situation, I turn on the radio to the 80's station. There's nothing more romantic than 80's music, but it's hard to listen to at a time like this. Hopefully nothing too romantic. The song "Wonderful Life" by Black comes on. I'd never heard it before but it's one of the most beautiful songs I've ever heard: the lyrics, synth, and calypso beat. I'm so moved yet feel so alone next to the girl who once loved me, but who I harmed greatly.

I look out over the beautiful sunset and then briefly make eye contact with Lilly. That and the beautiful melodic rhythms bring me to tears. For the rest of the drive home we don't exchange a single word. She just drops me off in front of my house and doesn't even say goodbye.

Chapter 10: This Man Has All The Answers

What have I done? Ruined my one chance at love with a sweet girl who accepted me for who I am, because I couldn't get over my silly adolescent obsessions. I get into some deep depression, deeper than what I experienced in high school with romantic rejection from girls who never even acknowledged my existence in the first place.

I spend hours alone in bed, in tears listening to 80's music. Then as the sadness subsides the eroticized rage sets in. I watch loads of porn, especially of Asian girls being utterly humiliated; barely legal Asian girls in sailor suits being ejaculated upon by multiple men. Is this my way of getting back at Lilly?

She's a decent person. She doesn't deserve that kind of humiliation. Her face deserves to stay sparkling clean, not covered in the ejaculate of tattooed parolees. I take a Klonopin to ease the eroticized rage. Then I stumble upon something online that really pierces the bottom of my soul. It's an excerpt from Noam's manifesto.

"I'm not an evil person. Really. I don't want to hate. I don't want to be stuck in this dark place of despair. All I ever wanted was just to have a sweet innocent girl, pure of heart, who could appreciate my sensitive, yet wounded soul. And there is that one girl waiting there for me. I can't even say her name, but I love her dearly and if I can't be with her then life has no purpose. I feel pity for any guy out there who had a shot at true love but screwed it up because they were too intellectually weak to understand that there is only one girl for every guy."

I always thought that this guy was a self-centered, egotistical, racist, misogynistic, scumbag but I can relate to his pain and suffering as a fellow wounded soul. But unlike him I was granted that one chance at love and blew it because of my own immaturity.

There's a sketch Noam did of the girl. No, this can't be. That blonde Jewish girl from my vision at the oasis who keeps reappearing.

I continue reading:

"There is a great man named Roger Blackstone. Some say he is a fascist. But I say he has all the answers. He can fix this cruel and unjust world. He will make sure that every lost soul stuck in the abyss will be granted the keys to operate the mechanisms that set one's place in this world. Mechanisms that are in the wrong hands, preventing me from achieving success, status, and most importantly to be with my one true love."

That girl. Is Noam trying to send me a message telepathically?

Lost for hope, I decide that the only solution is to find Blackstone and seek his guidance about social status, love, sex, politics, aesthetics, and how they all intersect, guiding me to the truth about life.

I've seen Blackstone's mansion from a distance up in the hills west of Alamo but I know it will be a daunting task to get in. As soon as it gets dark, I sneak out and order an Uber to drop me off in an exclusive residential neighborhood of Tudor and French Chateau style mansions in Alamo. The neighborhood security guard gives me a suspicious look, so I take an extra Klonopin to calm my angst.

I walk past the mansions and get to the base of the hills. The entire area surrounding Blackstone's estate was originally intended to become some development of McMansions but Blackstone bought out the developer and has much of the oak woodlands set aside as the Blackstone Preserve.

I look up and can see the general vicinity of where Blackstone's mansion is but realize it will be a daunting task to climb up. The first step is getting over the fence which separates the neighborhood from Blackstone's property. In his world only attractive females can cross the gate and enter utopia. While usually I'm petrified of heights, my motivation and extra Klonopin allows me to get over the fence. But damn it hurts my soft hands and weak muscles.

I must be strong if I want to face the one man who has all the answers to life's questions. The hills are covered in grass and oak woodlands but it's going to be a steep climb. Luckily there's a full moon to highlight my path. I take another Klonopin and run for it. I keep getting stuck in the grass and trip on one of the oak branches, almost falling down to a certain death.

Once I get close to the top my body is exhausted but my mind and soul are on fire. I breathe in the fresh dry fragrant air. Looking down, I can see a light far out watching over me. Must be the beacon of Mount Diablo.

I was expecting a massive impenetrable gate, but I find myself in a magical setting. Beyond the oak woodlands I find myself in Blackstone's private yard. There is a swimming pool, surrounded by lush vegetation and marble statues with the moonlight illuminating the water along with a bluish turquoise light permeating from inside.

What a hypocrite for his pool act tax on private pools. Imagine all the wild pool parties Blackstone hosts. Perhaps he's just another douchebag womanizer and not the wise sensitive man I was looking for. Either way I have to meet him to find out.

"Hands behind your back!"

A bright flashlight hits me right in the eyes. Oh great, it's the cops.

I feel handcuffs being put on me, straining my arms and back. I notice two men in black uniforms with the Blackstone logo on their patches. They must be Blackstone's private security detail.

I scream "where are you taking me?"

They don't respond. At this point I would be relieved if it actually were the cops. Maybe they're going to use me for some ritual human sacrifice where a bunch of debauched billionaires bid on who gets to snuff me. The security guards blindfold me so that I don't know the details of Blackstone's mansion.

They drag me off with my feet dangling on the marble floors. When they remove the blindfold, I find myself in the most magnificent room with crimson carpeting, and Mid-Century furnishings, including opulent yet tasteful clocks and light fixtures.

While I'm distracted checking out the aesthetics, I'm startled by the security guard taking out his walkie talkie, "he's here boss."

A tall slender man enters who I recognize as Roger Blackstone. He has wavy blonde hair, a pointy nose, round glasses, wearing a silk kimono, just like he did as a boy in my dream, and he's holding a cup of sake.

Blackstone asks "who do we have here? A trespasser."

The guard replies "we caught him sneaking in."

Blackstone scolds the guards for not doing their job and looks me straight in the eyes and orders me "down on your knees."

One of the guards puts a gun to my head as I get on my knees.

Blackstone starts to open up his kimono, fondling himself, while staring at me sadistically. Will my first sexual experience be fellating my political hero?

I awkwardly make eye contact with him while down on my knees. Then Blackstone bursts out laughing, "I'm just fucking with you lad. It's an old prank I picked up at a British Boarding School.

Blackstone takes me to his lounge. I sit down on his Mid-Century Modern sofa and he politely offers me a sake. I accidently hold the cup the wrong way and he demonstrates the proper etiquette that he learned in Japan.

Blackstone notices me staring at his art collection ranging from Italian Futurism, Surrealism, and 80s cyberpunk prints. He mentions that one particular piece is Jim Buckels' illustration from the 80's of a surreal utopia, a lake with archeo-futuristic architecture. He adds that he modeled his pool and garden on Buckels' "Ledas Bath" and I can see eerie similarities to my visions as well.

The purple mountain in the background must be Mount Diablo and there's even a full moon like tonight. Tonight, was my destiny, a fulfilled prophecy.

I awkwardly say, "I can now understand how you concoct all your visions."

"Aesthetic chaos magic," Blackstone jokes.

Then he shows me some art nude photos of blonde teenagers swimming in an alpine lake by some Avant Garde photographer. Blackstone goes on to say that he vacationed at that lake in Bavaria as a teenager in the 80's.

Those guys from the photo were from my vision of the oasis. Overwhelmed, I awkwardly respond "first of all my name is Max, Max von Mueller."

Blackstone responds "I know Max. I've been waiting for you. Ever since I saw you in that dream."

He must be really fucking with me for trespassing. He continues "there was this girl. My first love. This one magical night we were walking along the waterfront, lanterns shining in the lake, alpine accordion music playing, and I finally got the courage to ask her out. Turns out she wanted me but had to return home as summer vacation had come to an end.

We had one last night together, where some guys who were vacationing with her from Chadsworth invited us to go skinny-dipping in the lake. But she ended up getting drunk and making out with one of the guys. She left the next day and I never saw her again. A few months later, on a cold rainy night in London at the Regents Palace Hotel my father was up to his usual occult antics. I rushed outside to Piccadilly Circus to escape. I looked onto the reflection of the Art Deco Roman themed neon sign of the Regents Palace in a puddle. Heartbroken, longing for love that I felt was so far away, I noticed another world of rolling golden hills and animated gold neon illuminating the grass from the night sky. I could hear my name called out "Roger."

It was her voice. Staring into the world on the other side, I was

consumed into a tunnel of light, rushing through gold

grasslands, and then into the oasis in the oak groves. The girl,

my first love was there. You were there too watching from

behind the trees. Except it wasn't the original lake. It was in

California."

I ask Blackstone if he has a photo of that girl.

Blackstone replies "no, but I have a sketching."

I ask, knowing the answer, "did you draw that of her?"

"No," he replies. "It is from the manifesto of Noam

Metzenbaum, of his crush Natalie Bloom."

I ask "did you ever try to search for her?"

Blackstone says "of course. I sent out my best private

investigators, but there is no record of Mr. Bloom ever having

a daughter. That means that you, Noam, and I all accessed that

same realm: the Vapor."

I ask: "how can that girl, Natalie, frozen in time, be both here, in Connecticut, and at the lake in Germany back in the 80's?"

Blackstone explains "you know how in dreams we pick up the puzzle pieces of our greatest joys and worst traumas? That girl exists when all the right puzzle pieces come together, beyond our concept of space and time. I found bits and pieces but have been trying to put them all together. Experimenting with my various projects. But material goods are not enough."

Blackstone goes on to explain that "the objective of politics is to create the type of society you want to live in but who needs politics when you can visualize your ideal world?"

I like the idea, but I've always felt unfree, just stuck in the abyss trying to sort out the puzzle pieces.

I ask Blackstone "what does it mean to be truly free?"

Blackstone explains that "true freedom is not simply being free to break the rules and social mores that society has thrust upon you. Rather, it's about achieving the mental strength and vision to live in your own utopia that fits your desires." He asks "do you feel free Max?"

I respond "my entire life I've always thought I was not free because of social rejection and fear of breaking society's rules. But what I now realize is that what I have been searching for all this time was to find that place that fits my needs, visions, and desires."

He responds "then you must utilize the full power of your mind to create your very own utopia. What is preventing you from getting to that place Max?"

Looking for answers I reply "fear."

Blackstone responds "you have been conditioned, to be meek, to be a slave. But I know you have a great gift. I've seen your visions. You can't go forth and put them into fruition until you free yourself."

Anxiously thinking of what to say I take out my bottle of Klonopin. Blackstone grabs the pill bottle, observes it and states: "I have something for you."

He walks over to his cabinet and takes out a glass jar full of some kind of substance. Then tells me to stick out my tongue and uses an eye dropper to put a few droplets under my tongue and orders me to hold it for a minute. As soon as it sets in, I immediately feel at ease; all anxieties, fears, and negative thoughts vanish.

Blackstone explains it's a rare substance which he named Vaporio that he discovered in the Amazon. Not only can it cure anxiety without any negative side effects or withdrawal symptoms it also allows one to be in touch with the deepest corners of the subconscious, to reach one's full intellectual and creative potential. Blackstone explains he could make a fortune off it, but already has more than enough money and that this substance is not fit for mass consumption.

With a newfound sense of cockiness, I further challenge him: "I like your idea of a utopia for elite visionaries. But how do I know this isn't some gimmick. Another real estate scheme to make a fortune off every possible market? You create housing developments for the wealthy, amusement parks, hotels, resorts, and casinos. How do I know this isn't just another, commercial, extension of that?

Blackstone responds "you're still living in that dream world. If you want to implement your visions you have to step out of the Vapor sometimes. I was an artist as a boy, but I was lucky to have wealthy parents to fund my endeavors. I got into real estate after my father handed over his casino in Las Vegas. The perfect place to experiment in creating fantasy utopias. I realized that the economic elite form taste in consensus and impose it on the masses who lack the vision. But once I was wealthy enough and no longer concerned for profits, I could implement my own visions. Las Vegas is a city for people to escape from reality, but my plan is to bring those visions to the entire nation. But of course, it is crucial to fund innovation and the arts. I want to give those with the greatest visions and ideas a chance to put them into fruition, and have a greater role in the economy.

My plan now: the spirit of my Presidential campaign is elite replacement theory. To lead a coalition of intellectuals, artists, and technological innovators into overthrowing the current elite: parasites, who are content managing the decline, extracting resources while creating nothing tangible, with no vision for a brighter future."

I ask if there is some occultist significance to the oasis.

Blackstone proclaims "Yes, Zephyr McMillion."

Zephyr was that cult leader from Scotland who had that compound in the foothills. His fascist New Wave music now has a cult following among Blackstone's supporters.

Blackstone explains: "I initially came to California to meet Zephyr to find the key to unlock the subconscious. Zephyr was trying to use the occult to access the subconscious—not just his own but that of others. He believed that the one who was master of mankind's subconscious realm was the master of the universe. Such a person could manipulate the masses into carrying out their will, all through their dreams and fantasies.

While I was in college, I met him at his night club venue in San Francisco: Prometheus. You would have loved it, Greco-

Roman themed with animated Neon. Zephyr would travel across the country and pick up all these blonde preppy teen groupies from wealthy suburbs and bring them back to his compound. He wanted to start a political revolution by breeding a new super race by mixing the best genes of the new elite with the most attractive youth from the existing one. Something fresh that would combine ancient occultist tradition with a futurist new order. Zephyr realized that in order to win a revolution you have to win over the youth of the elite and turn them against their parents."

I ask Blackstone "what's the correlation between you, Zephyr, and fascism?"

Blackstone explains "it all goes back to my father, Alistair. We were from an old aristocratic family. My father was cut out of his inheritance due to publicly humiliating the family with his occultist rituals but was able to emerge as an Avant Garde artist in 60's London. He later became disillusioned with the counterculture and came to the conclusion that this new elite could not arise through either capitalism or liberalism. He viewed fascism as a vehicle for the innovators and creative visionaries to seize power from the gatekeepers. He ran for UK Prime Minister as the Beatnik Fascist but allegations came up about some violent occultist ritual and he fled the country, turned away from politics, and made a fortune in Las Vegas on the belief that his Aristocratic Radical ideals needed a place with no social standards and easy capital like Vegas to take hold.

I later rediscovered my father's ideas after meeting Zephyr who was influenced by him. Zephyr was also influenced by Oscar Wilde's philosophy of aestheticism. Like Wilde, Zephyr viewed politics as the artform of presenting a clear vision of the world through aesthetics. Beauty, he thought, was beyond good and evil, transcending all morality, and the bourgeoise work ethic. Originally a man of the left, Zephyr wanted to do away with the cutthroat competition of capitalism and replace it with a leisure economy where all are liberated to pursue their dreams with an open exchange of intellectual and creative endeavors."

"I like all these aesthetic visions but what is it with all the Nazi eugenics?" I ask.

Blackstone responds "Zephyr would often joke that some kind of genetically altered virus to eradicate the excess population of proles, like the Black Death, was necessary to prevent the incoming neo-feudal order. That was a bit too far, even for me, but what did intrigue me was his belief that class oppression was a product of aesthetic inequality, that so many people were denied access to beauty and that the hypercompetitive nature of capitalism was a result of competition over aesthetics. Zephyr gave up on any notion of egalitarianism and decided to handpick the most attractive youth from the wealthy to breed a new race to populate his utopia. The concentration of beauty currently exists in small pockets within the upper class and the declining fertility rates of this class promises even greater scarcity in the future. Zephyr wanted to create a world where everyone was attractive so we could do away with class altogether. To expand beauty, though, one would risk infringing upon the rights of the masses and garnering the opposition of the current elite who benefit from its scarcity. Zephyr's idea was that in order to redistribute wealth you'd have to take the most attractive sperm and eggs from the wealthy and implant them in the proletariat. With technologies such as artificial wombs and genetic engineering to delay ageing, Zephyr's eugenic ideals have become scientifically viable, yet the social taboos remain in place.

I can assure you that the elites backing DCR are also invested in gene editing technologies to use for nefarious aims like weeding out non-conformity, but with the campaign I'm presenting more humane and politically palatable solutions to the problems Zephyr controversially addressed. Zephyr read the section of my father's manifesto predicting that our entire economy will eventually be automated, with most menial jobs becoming obsolete. In that same section, my father advised that we have a limited time-frame before this singularity goes into effect. The new elite must seize the means of production before it's too late. They must use AI and the revenue generated from automation to advance civilization.

"What happened to Zephyr?" I ask.

He was prosecuted for crimes of a sexual nature and fled to Brazil as a fugitive where I met up with him a decade later in the Amazon to search for the substance. Once I discovered Vaporio things became clearer. I could analyze each of my visions without being consumed by any one of them. Blackstone points to a gilded Art Deco statue.

"Our situation—we the true visionaries—is analogous to one from Greek mythology. We are in lineage with Prometheus: the Greek god who enlightened mankind, giving them the secrets of Olympus. Our spiritual adversaries—the gatekeepers trying to access the secrets of the Vapor—are today's Olympians. They want the utopia all to themselves, the knowledge and beauty included, and to permanently close it off to the rest of mankind. Prometheans and Olympians exist today, you see, and are as locked as ever in a spiritual war."

I ask: "so where do I come in?"

Blackstone says "In the Vapor, your deepest desires will consume you, and if you stay there for long enough, you will be overwhelmed by aesthetic prowess and know of no right nor wrong. I have spent too much time there, but you haven't been totally corrupted. When the time comes you will know what to do."

I ask: "you want me to re-enter the Vapor?'

Blackstone responds "yes, I need you to find that girl for me. If you find her, I will turn your life around. Anyhow I have a meeting I need to get to, but you will know when the time comes."

Then he hands me some 80's aviator glasses, like the ones he wore as a boy in my dream. He says that he bought them at a souvenir shop at the lake in Bavaria in the 80s on the day he met her, and that they help him see the world more clearly. He orders his chauffer in a Blackstone automobile to escort me back home. Looking out the car window, I can see the clouds

down below, beautiful colors. Is it already sunrise?

Chapter 11: Abducted

Waking up the next day, I have no recollection of Blackstone's chauffeur dropping me off at home. Just another crazy dream. But wait: the aviators. Blackstone's a great man who knows things the rest of us can barely comprehend. He saw great potential in you. You actually are brilliant. You just need the courage and confidence to go forth. The mental power to shape your surroundings, rather than letting your surroundings determining your worth.

I'm ready to head back to school and face my fears about running into my ex-girlfriend Lilly, Natasha, and the douchey Art Bro Blake, and I shall use my newfound knowledge to succeed in academia.

I see Lilly in my Environmental Journalism class. I smile at her, but she ignores me. That's ok. I shall give her time to heal.

I head off to my Broadcasting class. I have what it takes to be the top newscaster for Blackstone Corp. rather than the Art Bro's bitch.

I get in my group. As usual Blake is flirting with Natasha. He orders me to go get him a coffee with soy milk and barks out "and it better not be crappy vending machine coffee; only organic, fair trade."

I rush off to the coffee kiosk but there's a long line.

When I get back to class, they're all gone. One student tells me my group is in the production studio.

I rush over to the studio, spilling some coffee on my polo.

When I get there, I see the group, except for Natasha and Blake, waiting outside. One of the students warns me that they are practicing, and I must stay out, but I explain I have to bring them their coffee.

A faint sound of moaning. Must be part of the script. But when I enter the studio and open the curtains, I find the two fornicating. Natasha screeches "get out pervert!"

She covers herself up and I briefly catch a glimpse of her shaven crotch. The Art Bro puts on his boxers. Wow, he's really well endowed.

I take the coffee and hand it to Blake, abruptly spilling it all over his bare chest.

When I get back to class to gather my belongings, I notice an emergency alert texted to me. I analyze it closely.

It says "Campus Security: you are in violation of sexual misconduct. Report to Campus Security immediately."

I take out my phone, obsessively checking social media, and realize my name has gone viral under #MeToo. I don't have to report to some meathead wannabe cop security officer. I'm beyond the slave morality of this decaying civilization. Blackstone saw greatness in me and now it's time for me to move on to greater things.

When I arrive home my dad has an announcement:

"Max, I've been laid off from my job. The situation has been difficult on the family and we can no longer afford to live here. My work offered me a severance package if I agreed to remotely train my replacement from Bangalore. I had no other option. I found a nice retirement community out in the country near Modesto. It's 50 and over, but I know the manager and he made an exception for you kids. You can live with us, but you must understand that we are retired now, and you must take responsibility for yourself. You are expected to get a job as soon as we get settled and not complain."

Modesto? What the fuck? My father just wants a cushy retirement. No regard for my future. Whether I get into a good university, find a high-status job, meet the girl of my dreams, and become culturally sophisticated. There's no culture or anything for me in bumfuck Modesto. I remember stopping there on the way to Yosemite as a boy and using a disgusting truck stop restroom where some old overweight trucker came on to me. I can really appreciate my home now. I got to hike in the hills nearby, eat the best gourmet cuisine, check out pretty girls, and head out to the City every now and then. And now it's all being taken away from me.

I would rather die than live in fucking Modesto. I should run away and go live with Blackstone. If that doesn't work, I can just camp out in the hills, steal organic vegetables from peoples' gardens, and bathe in their pools.

After a couple of uneventful weeks, we head off to Modesto. I get one last glimpse of Mount Diablo, then we head off over the Altamont Pass, past the Wind Farms towards the vast San Joaquin Valley. It now hits me that everything I so cherished is behind me and that a bleak future awaits. When we're still young we hold on to that dream of what the good life will be. As we reach adulthood we desperately cope to hold on to that dream, but it slips away when faced with the harshness of reality.

Suddenly a chopper starts hovering up above. That's one thing from my past that unfortunately I can't leave behind. Once you've been designated a potentially dangerous social outcast, they will watch you till your grave.

The wind turbine covered rolling golden hills give way to a vast flat terrain of farmland which goes on as far as the eye can see but the air's filled with dust and grime, making it hard to see out into the distance.

As we get off the highway, I notice the high-speed rail under construction is financed by Blackstone Inc. I wonder if it will bring civilization to this shithole or just create more sprawl for useless eaters to breed more stupid ugly people. Past Downtown Modesto there's some rundown ghetto areas, then a suburban area which seems more middle class, and then out to the outskirts of town were in the distance I can see the rolling golden hills reminding me of the beautiful scenery I left behind.

We pass a golf course and enter our gated community. This is far worse sprawl and waste of resources than anything I've seen in the Bay Area and the sizes of the homes here are massive; especially compared to our modest house. How could my parents squander my inheritance on this garbage?

I look around the retirement community and it seems deserted except for a disgusting overweight older man in a Hawaiian shirt with his younger Southeast Asian wife. Probably cashed out on his 401(k) to SEAmaxx. These McMansions must be filled with lots of old people from the Bay Area who sold their homes to foreign investors and left their own children with nothing. There are no hot girls here either. Just useless old misers living here in this un-aesthetically pleasing ecologically unsustainable wasteland, exploiting people of color.

I walk around our minimalist McMansion and head off to my massive new bedroom which even has a private bathroom. We even have a guest room, a massive kitchen with a stainless-steel fridge, and a TV room. Who needs all this when we'll likely never have guests?

The next day I wake up in a sense of dread. This is my life from now on. Every day just sitting alone in this big house. Stacey will probably go off to college. I'll be forced to get some stupid minimum wage job. Wasted potential with no chance to get out. Already bored to death sitting around the house for several hours, I decide to see if there's any urban life in this town.

I take a Klonopin and head off on my bike toward downtown to check out the scene. There are some historic buildings of interest and some attempts at urban renewal but for the most part downtown is full of parking lots, fast food joints, seedy dive bars, and boarded up storefronts. With all the sprawl there seems to be little interest in investing in urbanism and improving the overall aesthetic.

Lots of thugmaxxers and lower class foids who appear to have several offspring each, breeding another generation of useless proles. Blackstone would, for sure, refuse to subsidize their unwanted pregnancies.

Walking around in the heat, I feel my stomach growl. I look around for places for lunch but see nothing but fast-food joints and dive bars. I finally find a Mexican restaurant which looks halfway decent. I order a cheese enchilada and a large horchata to quench my thirst. I feel a bit guilty for my bigoted thoughts after interacting with the friendly older LatinX woman who serves me lunch. You can't be an elitist. The capitalists want you to look down on others. Be a leader for the proletariat. And besides, these underprivileged foids will be impressed by your pedigree, JBW. I thank the server, leave a 5-dollar tip, and walk out with my head up, knowing that I must face my challenges in stride.

Before I head back home, I stumble upon some cool retro theater with a neon marquee: a sign of civilization. Perhaps this place does have potential.

Chapter 12: Wage Cuck

The next day while sleeping in, my father bursts into my room to wake me up.

"You thought you could just come here and laze away? He says. "It's time for you to go out and get a job Max. I heard they're hiring at Walmart."

I respond "Walmart? Fucking Walmart? You brought me up in a nice upper middle-class lifestyle. I tried hard to fit in, and get good grades so I could attain social status, and you waste all our money, and leave me to rot. Fuck you!"

My father shouts "you ungrateful little brat. Now go get dressed, get out, and I expect you to have a job interview scheduled by the time you return."

There's no fucking way I'll work at Walmart. After all the hard work I put into high school, trying hard to become culturally sophisticated, and my newfound sense of greatness granted to me by Roger Blackstone. Working as a lowly slave for the capitalists I so deeply despise. I'd rather run off into the Sierras and work on my manifesto for reshaping civilization, but I need my morning shower and coffee.

Dad orders me out the door. I get on my bike and head off to Walmart. Sold off into slavery. I walk past the massive parking lot to the ugly Walmart. What a waste. Whoever built this should be tried for crimes against aesthetics. I ask one of the staff for a job application, I fill it out, and submit. I should really try to screw it up, so I don't get stuck here. Just spending 10 minutes here makes me depressed.

The next week I spend all my time indoors browsing the internet, looking over my photos, and keeping up with the election and Roger Blackstone. Blackstone has a new campaign add targeting California voters called "Vaporfornia."

It starts with footage of grand building projects from the past such as the Panama Pacific International Exposition and the Golden Gate Bridge in SF with the caption "We once dreamt big and built it." Then an image of a family from the 50s moving into a new Mid-Century Modern home and blonde teenagers surfing on the beach with the caption "and we lived well." Then footage of declining public schools, gridlocked freeways, abandoned malls, and ageing wealthy communities, culminating with a NIMBY protest against one of Blackstone's projects with the caption "We lost the dream, yet we resist a brighter future." There's a couple in a Blackstone automobile driving down a highway through the golden hills. They just missed the turn with a sign that says "To a brighter future." The golden hills then turn into an area of blighted strip malls with the caption "you took the wrong turn but it's not too late. Make a U-Turn back, and get to that brighter future." The couple end up swimming at Blackstone's Oasis Resort and then having sunset cocktails at his Plaza Hotel in SF.

The product placement is great. Even with the racist dog whistles. Blackstone perfectly articulates his vision through aesthetic imagery. It's going to be a close race with a lot of progressives refusing to buy into DCR's woke capitalism. The media keeps calling them enablers of fascism for refusing to back the Democratic nominee. Perhaps a taste of fascism is what's needed to wake up the bourgeoise. Jackson's not too popular with much of the conservative base either. Rightwing trolls call him a cuckservative.

Sleeping in one day, I realize it's my first job interview. I quickly get ready and head off to Walmart. The manager interviewing me is a LatinX man who must be over 300 lbs. My anxiety causes me to try my best, while my Klonopin takes a little off the edge of my social awkwardness. So much for my plan to fuck things up.

A week later I get an email that says I've been accepted to stock merchandise for minimum wage. All my youthful aspirations and ideals crushed. Stuck here until I'm middle aged. I look around at my co-workers and customers. I feel as out of place here as I did with the popular crowd at my high school. Not accepted by those with social status within society, thrown away like garbage, yet even the proles won't accept me with open arms. Perhaps I really am of that natural elite Blackstone was referring to in our conversation. Nah, just delusional thinking. But I finally realize now the real reason I resented other White people so much growing up. It was not because of my White privilege as my teachers had taught me. That was just a coping mechanism to deal with my own feelings of inadequacy.

The truth is I resented the rich popular guys for not accepting me, and the hot popular girls for not dating me. Therefore, I viewed persons of color as my fellow underdogs who were oppressed just like me. But in fact, I viewed them more as sacred objects rather than as actual human beings who have their own base desires. My father's asshole conservative mentality calling everyone who failed in the capitalist system a lazy bum didn't help either.

But what makes you think you're entitled to the best aesthetics? Especially without putting in the hard labor these people of color so desperately put in. That's what the capitalists want you to think. But then: I am the the one with those visions that inspired Blackstone.

I close my eyes and try to come back to my senses. My supervisor interrupts my maladaptive daydreaming and orders me to spend the rest of my shift stocking merchandize to feed the obese overfed proles. A job outdated and soon to be automated.

While riding home on my bike, I pass by fruit orchards and some shacks where the farmworkers live. As I continue daydreaming about what my life could have been, I notice a group of LatinX teenagers blocking the path. I should just ride right by them. But I'm surrounded. Panicking, I get off my bike as the guys start approaching me with a look of intimidation.

Their leader asks, "what you doin here White boy?"

I try to avoid making eye contact and continue on my way.

Their leader shouts "listen ese! You on our turf!"

I explain "I just moved to the area. Now please, I have to get home."

One guy interrogates me, "you moved into one of those new mansions ese?" I nod yes.

He says "you on stolen land. This is Mehico. Occupied Territory. Those old rich White fools come in and treat us like slaves. Without our labor they'd be livin in trailer parks." I flinch as he gets close to my face.

Their leader proclaims "We the Harnizos! You best be respecting our turf."

Then he kicks my bike over, and they all laugh. I quickly pull it back up, get on, and ride past them as fast as I can so that they can't find out where I live, but I'm terrified that this incident took place so close to my home.

As much as I despise those thugs, they did have a point. Those greedy old bastards hire all these undocumented immigrants to exploit, and they end up creating more criminal offspring. Then the old White people lock themselves away in their gated compound to segregate themselves from what they created.

I go home and Google the term Harnizo to find out if they are a dangerous criminal organization. I find nothing about their gang but find pictures of douchey looking actors and male models—Chadriguez's as the incels call them—posted on some bizarre web forum that fixates on ethno-phenotypes. The website claims that a Harnizo is a LatinX person who is around 60-75% Spaniard and 40-25% Indigenous Mexican. But these dudes were nothing like those actors and models from the website. These were outright criminal thugs, and I know that if they catch me wandering around on their turf again I'm dead.

Petrified of leaving the house, I stay indoors all day and night. I even call my work and use the few sick days I have so I don't have to leave the house, risking running into them again. When Blackstone takes power, we will have a leisure economy with two month long paid vacations, spending our Blackstone bucks at his erotic resorts. I find my Swiss Army Knife that my grandfather gave me as a boy as protection

against the Harnizos. If they fuck with me, I'll just stab em'
dead right in their hearts.

I tell my parents that I'm sick. My mother understands but my
father goes off on another angry drunken rant that I can't
handle a hard day's work just like all the other lazy entitled
youth who are bankrupting this nation. After going crazy from
being indoors so long, I head out for an evening stroll to
breath in the warm dusty air.

To avoid the path near the orchards where the Harnizos were, I
walk on the golf course instead. Some old fat golfer yells at
me to get out of his way. I flip him off and tell him to "drop
dead old fuck! "His dumbfounded reaction is priceless. I don't
think I've ever cursed someone out like that before but life
here seems to be pretty meaningless so I might as well say
what I please.

Chapter 13: Mouse Trap

I find myself back near the orchards as it's getting late. A group of guys are approaching me in the distance but I can't make out who they are. Better not be the Harnizos. Terrified, I stare off into the orchards. Then I hear steps approaching me. I look down to the ground and then look up. Luckily it's not the Harnizos but these are some really scary dudes. Skinheads with swastikas carved into their foreheads, just like Charles Manson.

Are they criminal thugs who want to beat me up or will they accept me for being of the same race? I meekly say "hello." There's dead silence as their leader slowly approaches me.

He asks: "who are you and what are you doing in these parts?"

I anxiously explain "my name is Max. Max von Mueller. I just moved here with my family from the Bay Area to get away from all the….…..." Flinching, as I almost said some horrible racial slurs.

He responds "chill. We accept you as a fellow White brother, but you must prove your worth."

I ask "do I need a swastika on my forehead?" .

One jokes you have to murder a Harnizo to earn that honor.

I ask: "can you please explain the significance of your magnificent organization?"

They give me weird looks. Probably think anyone who talks with an intellect is LGBTQ.

Their leader proclaims "we are GAJOCAMI; Goyim Against Jewish Oligarchic Control And Mestizo Invasion. It's pronounced 'Juajocami'."

I joke "sounds Spanish."

One guy explains that "some of us have Mexican girlfriends or moms and pick up the lingo but they still got to go."

Their leader tells him to shut the fuck up. I tell them my story that "the other night I was going for a pleasant evening stroll, when a group of Harnizos viciously verbally assaulted me and threatened me with physical abuse."

One guy says "this isn't SF. You can't survive here if you act like a little bitch. We got your back, but you need to learn how to fight."

I've never been in a fight in my entire life, but I lie and say "I once stabbed a person of color who tried to rob me and assault my Aryan girlfriend."

I feel like scum for betraying all my core principles and everything I was taught growing up but surprisingly they bought my story and their leader says: "welcome to GAJOCAMI."

I now feel a sense of belonging to a tribe, no longer caste aside, and empowered by having the comradery of these powerful strong men. Now I can understand why lower-class thugs are so cocky, despite being at the bottom of society.

I ask them "what do you think about Roger Blackstone?"

Their leader explains "I know a lot of White Nationalist are shilling for Blackstone but they're all grifters. Blackstone's campaign's just another Kosher Astroturf with Rothschild ties in his family going way back. He's not for White revolution and if you're a Blackstone fanboy you can't join our crew."

Maybe these guys aren't my crowd. They're not the most culturally sophisticated but I need to join a tribe if I want to survive and not end up gang raped by the Harnizos.

I've been rethinking everything I learned about racism and White privilege in school. The thing is capitalism creates a scarcity mindset and forces us all to compete for scarce resources. DCR is wrong that woke capitalism and criminalizing hate speech will end inequality and Blackstone has been saying that giving everyone a monthly check will ease racial tension. I mustn't feel guilty about bigoted thoughts and slurs and realize that I too am also a victim of the neoliberal system, and that capitalism is responsible for any horrible racist thoughts that I may think in times of scarcity.

As I come home for dinner, I can hear yelling from indoors. As soon as I open the door, I overhear my dad shouting "my daughter's dating a worthless thug!" My mom tries to calm him down.

He shouts, "I'll murder that fucker if he comes anywhere near our house!" Eventually he just leaves, slamming the door.

My mom's in the kitchen making dinner. She asks me to set the dinner table for "our guest."

I already feel sick to my stomach. I sit down and sip a glass of local Central Valley wine. Not Napa quality but good enough to calm my nerves. The doorbell rings. My sister walks in with her new boyfriend. It's one of the Harnizos. He acts all friendly shaking my hand and thanking my mom for her hospitality, acting oblivious to the fact that he harassed me earlier. He's also dressed up to look respectable with his tattoos covered by long sleeves. My dad left so he won't make a scene. But maybe he was right not to want this creep around the house.

At dinner my mom fauns over him, completely ignoring me. He doesn't bother talking to me either, and why would he? A violent criminal who tried to threaten me is right here in my very own home. After dinner my sister and the Harnizo head upstairs. I can tell something bad could happen.

I confront my mom "how can you let that dirty criminal into our home? Are you out of your fucking mind?"

My mom protests "you should be happy for your sister. Just because he is of a different race doesn't mean he's a criminal. I thought I taught you better than that."

I rush upstairs to my sister's room and put my head to the door to eavesdrop. I can hear muffled talking but fear the worst. This is so fucked up. I don't even want to think what could happen. I hear my mom walking up the stairs, so I head back to my room. All worst-case scenarios playing in my head. No don't picture that. Overcome with nausea, I rush to my bathroom and try to vomit but nothing comes out. After my nausea subsides, I start to think things through. I have no idea if anything happened, but I need to make sure that fucker never comes near our house again.

The next day I run into the skinheads. In distress I tell the leader "my sister was raped!"

The leader asks, "who did it?"

I'm hesitant to tell but he shouts: "who the fuck did it?"

I explain "it was a Harnizo."

He responds "don't worry. We're gonna take care of that little bitch."

I fantasized about murdering that piece of crap, but shit is about to get real. I don't want to go to prison as an accomplice to murder.

I head back home, and everyone acts like everything is normal. My dad's watching TV and drinking beer, my mom's cooking and organizing the family photo album, and my sister's texting her friends from back home.

A few days later I wake up to my sister crying. My mom runs upstairs to check on her, and I follow her to the door to eavesdrop.

My mom asks, "what's wrong dear?"

My sister continues to sob. Eventually she explains that her boyfriend Fernando was hospitalized in a coma after a brutal assault. She further explains that he's in a public hospital and that the only way to save his life is to raise funds to get him transferred to a private one. She begs my mom for financial support but my mom says, "I need to consult with your father."

My sister shouts "dad's a fucking racist! He wanted this."

My mom breaks down sobbing, "How could you say that. Your dad loves you a lot."

I feel a bit of schadenfreude after what I was put through, absolutely ecstatic that the piece of garbage got what he deserved, but this will destroy my family and worst of all, what if it's linked to me and I am tried as an accomplice for assault and attempted murder?

I spend the next day in my room alone with my thoughts, even with the pills I'm in panic.

I keep reassuring myself that I did not request for him to be beaten up. They acted on their own intuition, but just being associated with Nazis makes you a criminal in the eyes of the law and respectable society.

After going insane from spending another couple of days alone indoors, I take an extra Klonopin and go out for an evening walk.

As I'm walking down the path by the orchards, I run into the skinheads. There's a helicopter hovering up above. Probably surveilling my affiliation with them to use as evidence in the trial.

I'm about to run off to hide but the leader, noticing me, says "we took care of the Harnizo who raped your sister. Now you got to pay up."

I explain "I don't have any money."

He shouts "look, we just put our asses on the line to defend your Aryan sister's honor. Now we expect $800 by the end of the week or you're in for a serious beat down."

I tell them I will get them their money ASAP but I have no clue where I'm going to come up with that much.

My parents canceled my credit card a while back because I would often splurge on gourmet meals at the finest restaurants and purchase rare vintage collectibles online. I once even splurged on reservations for a five-star resort in Napa in hopes of asking out this cute popular girl in my history class, but never got the courage to talk to her and the reservation was wasted. Now I only have about $40 in cash.

I rush home desperate for ideas as to how I can come up with that kind of money. I could sure use some of those Blackstone bucks; 2000 a month if you're an artist, writer, or blogger. 1000 for everyone else. And state subsidized colonies for the intelligent but poor. Creative visionaries who lack the opportunities and credentials like me.

That would solve a lot of my problems, I'd be able to eat gourmet cuisine, travel sometimes, and have no need to work some dead-end job. But Blackstone isn't in office and I need the money now.

I consider all the possibilities; I could donate my sperm, but I probably won't pass the screening process, not mentally fit to pass on my genes. Or I could sell one of my kidneys but with all the pills I'm taking I'll probably need them. I could sell Blackstone's aviators, but they are the one thing I have that connects me to something greater. Then I overhear something.

My dad comforts my mom and tells her how much he loves her and how bad he feels for expressing rage at her and the family due to stress form financial problems. He reminisces about how he worked all summer as a caddy at the country club to save up to buy her a diamond wedding ring from some antique jewelry store in San Francisco.

I feel horrible about myself, but I have no other option. I'm going to steal that ring, sell it, and then pay off the skinheads to stay alive.

Feeling sick from what I'm about to do, I vomit in a trash bin in the hallway. My mom notices and tells me to get some rest and asks me if there's anything she can get me such as ginger ale or Pepto-Bismol. I feel even more disgusted with myself. I shouldn't have allowed my bigotry, toxic masculinity, and illusions of greatness consume me.

The next day while my parents are gone on their first date in a long time, and my sister is out who knows where, I take a bunch of Klonopin to numb my guilt and sneak into my parents' master suite to steal the ring. I admire how magnificent it is: an exquisite work of artistry.

The engraving says Blackstone Corp. Probably used child slave labor at their diamond mines in Africa. All that bullshit about being a poor downtrodden artist. The Blackstone's are just capitalist imperialistic scum. But it's still the perfect ring.

They don't make rings like that anymore with all the mass-produced junk from China. The type of ring I would give to my future wife if I could ever achieve that kind of status. But marriage is only for the wealthy now. I have to become a multimillionaire and right now I can hardly keep my crap job at Walmart.

I take the ring and head off to a pawn shop downtown. I hand it to an Arab man who can barely speak English. He hands me $950 for the ring which is probably worth at least $2000. Just enough money left over to buy lunch for the next week.

I hand over the cash to the skinheads in a paper lunch bag. They are satisfied and their leader says that I have potential to be a warrior for the race.

When I arrive home, everyone is flipping out; my sister's in tears, my dad is shouting, and my mom is trying to calm down the situation. Did they figure out I stole the ring? I screwed up big time.

Mom says to my sister "don't worry. They won't hurt you."

I'm confused and ask: "what's going on?"

My dad tells me "stay the fuck out of the way. We're in serious danger."

My mom says "he needs to know." She explains "Max dear, when your sister's boyfriend was in a coma, some criminals suspected that your father had something to do with it, and threatened violence against our family. Your sister is so scared she can't even leave the house."

Suddenly I hear a big bang. A brick smashes into the large glass window overlooking the dining room; broken glass shattering everywhere.

Dad shouts, "everyone. Get the hell upstairs! I'm taking care of this."

I look out my window and see the Harnizos right in front of our house. I feel terrified that my selfish actions put our family in mortal danger.

Then I hear a gun shot and the Harnizos run off. The cops show up about 20 minutes later. I take several pills and don't wake up until the next morning.

I want to find out what went down last night but have to rush off to work since all my sick days are used up. No time for coffee, or to use the bathroom. I can't use a disgusting Walmart toilet so I'll just have to hold it in all day.

Chapter 14: The Black Pill

I spend the next few hours at work stalking merchandise. Lots of annoying announcements and cheesy pop songs on the speakers. Then the 80's song "Heaven Is a Place on Earth" starts playing, reminding me of my breakup with Lilly, which almost brings me to tears. I ponder what my life could have been if I made things work with her and didn't have to move away. I will never get to experience that ever again.

I want to burst out in tears, all alone in this unaesthetically pleasing environment, stocking crappy merchandise, listening to the annoying customers. I have no one here I can connect to. I need just one person I can commiserate with. As I start breaking down in tears, a group of ugly lowlifes walk by laughing at me.

In rage, I knock all the merchandise off the shelves, making a big bang. My supervisor comes by to check on the situation. I explain it was an accident, but he says that if it happens again he will have to write me up.

I feel so humiliated having to take orders from someone who is way beneath my intellect. Yes, I have the intellect, but lacked the opportunities to utilize it and succeed in this world.

I look down the other aisle and see a megaphone. I grab it and try to turn it on but accidentally break it. Then I throw it on the ground, smashing it.

I take another megaphone, try to get it to work while trying to avoid being seen.

After managing to get it to work, I do some silent "la la la's" which some Australian spiritual guru on YouTube said would help with oratory skills.

Some cute LatinX teen girls get creeped out, thinking I made a crude oral sex gesture at them. They are too prole to be worthy of that anyhow. In Blackstone's world that act is a luxury reserved for rich girls.

I turn on the megaphone and announce "listen up proles. I'm here to establish a new aristocratic order. A new Imperium!"

I point to all the merchandise, "look at all this rubbish. The capitalists become richer producing more crap made by slaves in sweatshops for you lowly dysgenic masses!"

Then I point to some ugly overweight man stuffing his face with Egg McMuffins, "chicklets are thrown into meat grinders as we speak just to feed you disgusting subhuman scum!"

I point to an obese woman covered in tattoos with her equally trashy husband and their three kids and shout "capitalism thrives on breading a lower quality of human, creating more consumers for the parasites." The man looks like he's about to attack me.

I see more workers stocking the aisle and shout "all your jobs are going to be automated! You slaves are nothing but obsolete equipment!"

As I continue knocking over merchandise, I notice several security guards about to apprehend me. I shout at them "you fucking slaves. You think you're tough now, but you too will be replaced by robots!"

They follow me as I run outside. Looking around at the ugly parking lot, I proclaim on the megaphone "look at all this waste. Crimes against aesthetics! You will all be held accountable for these crimes!"

I hear police sirens, and realize I'm going to jail with thugs much worse than those Harnizos.

When I regain consciousness, I don't even remember getting arrested. Must have blacked out from the stress and hot sun.

I awake in a small concrete cell feeling drugged. Probably put on some anti-psychotics after my mental breakdown. I'd rather be drugged on Klonopin, not this crap. I can't take this, "get me out of here!"

I break down sobbing. Caged like a feral animal. Feeling claustrophobic, I start panicking, the drugs making me feel dizzy. Don't think I can make it. I try to meditate to find some semblance of peace with my situation. Never thought I'd ever actually end up in a place like this.

After waiting alone in the cell for what seems like several hours, I have a visitor. A social worker explains that I have been committed for my incident and reminds me of my privilege saying, "if you weren't White you'd be in jail." If jail is worse than this, then kill me.

She explains that the parents of the children that I terrified with my rant are considering pressing charges of child endangerment, and that it's important to be in touch with mental health professionals in case they do decide to press charges. She adds that I've been put on a 48 hour hold.

The next day is miserable, constantly drugged on crappy cheap meds and not able to eat their disgusting food.

Finally, an orderly comes by to inform me that my parents are downstairs to pick me up. There's dead silence on the ride home from the asylum.

I rush up to my room to cry, realizing I'm not the great visionary that Blackstone convinced me that I was. I should have listened to those who warned me about that con man.

Should have stayed in my lane and not allowed illusions of grandeur to turn me into a psychopath.

I expected my dad to yell at me for losing my job and embarrassing the family, but he continues to spend every day getting drunk, watching cable news on his new big screen. He's given up on me having a future so why bother getting angry. He's retired now and wants to relax and my mom's too busy making sure that my sister stays out of trouble.

I'm an adult so I have to fend for myself. But I was never granted the opportunities or skills to navigate this cruel world. This is my life from now on. This is it. No point in having dreams. Better to benzomaxx and numb the misery. I take several more pills and pass out. When I wake up the next day, I realize I'm getting low. My refills won't be available for a while so I'm in for some severe withdrawal symptoms.

It's not just the severe depression but also horrible flu-like symptoms of nausea and muscle cramps. What is my future? Will I just stay here and rot until my parents become elderly?

My sister will go off to college and become a party girl, my dad will just get fatter and drunker, and my mom will just give up on me as well. Why don't I just end it all now and rope. Take myself out of this misery. No one even bothers to check on me. They have their own problems.

I wish I could hunt down and murder every single adult who told me I could amount to great things when I was a boy. All lies. Our entire society is based upon the big lie, the so-called American dream, to keep the workers working and the consumers buying more junk. Take the Black Pill and realize that there's no movie ending, no girl from my dreams there waiting for me once I ascend, and there's no fucking oasis. All my visions were just a cope: fantasies of something I will never experience. Even if I had studied hard, got into a good school, and careermaxxed.

About a week later my mom picks up my Klonopin refill from the pharmacy. When I take the first pill, I can feel all the negative energy leave my mind and body, my muscle cramps and nausea gone. I feel liberated, but I know things won't get better. I can take action now. Maybe that world from my dreams is awaiting me in the afterlife. That other dimension Blackstone was talking about.

I step out onto the balcony and look out over the golf course, past the fruit orchards, the rolling golden hills and further out to the outline of the Sierras in the haze, and the Tuolumne River which originates up in the high country of Yosemite, reminding me of all the trips I took there as a boy. If I'm going to end this pathetic life once and for all I must see Yosemite one last time.

While my dad is off golfing and my mom is at the grocery store, I steal his keys and go to the garage and get in his Ford Mustang Shelby gt35. One of those things he splurged on to relive his youth instead of investing in my future. He'll probably be more upset about his precious automobile than his own son.

I can't drive, but that's ok. Played enough driving games and if the cops pull me over I'll take them on a lethal car chase.

Drive right into a ravine. Go out with a bang, not a whimper as society had intended.

I rev up the engine. The vibration of the car under my balls gets me hard. If I had a date she'd be wet by now. But none of that matters.

I start driving around. Almost hit an elderly couple getting out of their brand-new Mercedes SUV. Fuck them. They've profited from this nation at its prime, looting it, leaving nothing for my generation. They've consumed more than their fair share. I should run them over for depriving me of a future.

I finally start to get the feel for driving. I'll be at Yosemite in no time. Luckily my neighborhood's gate is open, and I zip right through. Onto the highway. Zipping right past the fruit orchards and grape vines. I can see the outline of the Sierras getting closer.

Wow, I feel like a man driving this car. If my parents had bought me a car for my 16th birthday maybe I would have had the confidence to ask out one of the popular girls and not have to resort to this. Anyhow, it's too late.

I take out my pill bottle and take two more Klonopin. Up the winding roads of the foothills. I had no idea how close I was, yet so far away.

Usually I'd feel terrified of driving off a cliff but since I'm going to die anyways, I have this intense confidence to drive through every curve. I roll down the window and breathe in the fresh pine scented air. Isn't life great?

I connect my phone's Bluetooth to the car and play a Vaporwave rendition of the Eurodance song "Castles in the Sky" that is slowed down perfectly to capture the essence of Hypnagogia. I will find my Castle in the Sky once I get to the other side. Just take in the music. Enjoy this last stretch of beauty. Perhaps there is no afterlife. Savor what you have left of this one.

Distracted, I swerve in front of a giant truck, which blares its horn. I swiftly drive out of the way, panicking, almost crashing into a ravine. I could have offed myself just then but less romantic than jumping off Glacier Point.

I pull over on to the shoulder and get out. I look out at the ravine and magical sunset over the majestic pines. Oh, how arriving at Glacier Point, watching Yosemite Valley at sunrise, and experiencing the pure essence of nature would have been so moving, yes spiritual, that it would bring me closer to God so that I would decide not to take my life. A moving story to tell my future grandchildren.

Maybe if I finish the bottle of Klonopin I'll have the courage to jump here. I'll probably just fall and injure myself and be stuck down there, dying a slow agonizing death.

The reality is you're a coward, a wimp. You don't even have the courage to drive up this damn mountain. That's the reason you've amounted to nothing in your life. Your intelligence and romantic visions mean shit.

This is still a nice spot though. Maybe I will just build a cabin and live out here. No worries, no status. Just me and nature.

It's getting dark soon and I won't be able to drive either up or down. I'll have to look for a place to eat, perhaps have a beer and figure out a plan in the morning. I remember seeing a sign for some tourist trap a few miles back. Must be one of those old gold mining towns.

I feel pretty high from the pills, but I will make it. But the engine won't start. Fuck! I forgot to fill up the tank. I'm so fucked but it's late now. I'll get some rest and figure things out in the morning.

Chapter 15: White Escalade

As I'm dozing off, I'm startled by a bright light. I look to the side and see a White Cadillac Escalade pulled up on the shoulder.

That's the one that's been following me. They followed me to Modesto and all the way up here. And will probably continue to haunt me in the afterlife.

Two men step out: an overweight middle aged bald man in a white suit and a younger thuggish looking man. I have no clue if they pulled over to help or to fuck with me. They're either undercover agents or some organized crime bosses. What could they possibly want from me? I stay in the car, trying to avoid making eye contact. Then startled by tapping on the door, I flinch.

I look for my Klonopin but am all out. Then I look to the side and see the two men laughing. I slowly open the door, trembling anxiously. The older fat man says, "you look like you had a rough night."

I put out my hand to shake, "Hi. I'm Max, Max von Mueller.

The fat man introduces himself as "Delmont Waverly."

The other man, looking me over, just says "Carson."

He looks to be in his 30's, has a shaved head, pierced ears, a goatee, and neck tattoo.

Delmont asks if I need any assistance and I explain that I was driving and ran out of gas.

Delmont asks, "where you headed?"

I stumble…. "well, I was leaving from….and might go over to."

Delmont asks, "you transporting narcotics?" I start shaking anxiously.

The two men burst out laughing again and Delmont pats me on the back, "you're with us now. We got the finest cocaine back at our motel. Get in and we'll call you a tow truck in the morning."

Noticing me shaking anxiously, Delmont drags me into the back seat and slams the door shut. I'm their captive now. But the thing is, if they were actually government agents, wouldn't they have a warrant and what possibly would some organized crime lords want from me? Just two guys who happen to drive a very common automobile, looking to help another man down on his luck. They go on about how much they're' going to drink and all the fine ladies at the tavern.

Once we get to the tavern there's an animated neon sign of a cowboy lassoing a bull. Very Lynchian, like something right out of Twin Peaks. There are rumors that David Lynch is a closet Blackstone supporter and that Blackstone is building a theme park called Lynchland but Lynch denies the rumors.

We enter the tavern which has an Old West theme with wooden walls with deer skulls, a mechanical bull, and loud country music playing. A waitress approaches Delmont as if

195

he were a VIP patron and takes us to the only empty red booth in the crowded restaurant. They both order barbequed ribs and shots of Jack Daniels and I order a salad with a wheat beer on tap.

Delmont asks "aren't you gonna try the ribs? They're the best in this state."

"No...I'm...ah, a vegetarian," I reply.

They burst out laughing. Delmont says "my boy Carson here's a vagitarius too. He loves eaten at the Y. The other night I walked in on him eating out some fat Mexican whore."

My salad arrives. It's nothing but iceberg lettuce, shredded carrots, and ranch dressing. Maybe I should have ordered the ribs because it might be my last meal. I sit there anxiously sipping my beer.

Delmont asks, "so what do you do Max?"

I respond, "I'm a journalist."

With a big creepy smile, Delmont takes a shot of Jack Daniels and says "you're a lucky boy. You see Max, I'm a producer. I produced a sports TV show back in Dallas." He asks, "you into politics?"

Don't mention Roger Blackstone. Playing it safe I say "yes, I'm a libertarian."

Delmont says "I'll let you in on a secret. An investor gave me $30 Million to set up a TV Station in Reno and we're collaborating with a big time Hollywood producer to create a premier entertainment show that covers politics." Perhaps it is Blackstone.

Delmont says "we're looking for a star to launch our station. The next great political pundit. Someone young, someone handsome."

He dips his fingers in the Jack Daniels, starts rubbing it along my lips, and then order me to "lick it."

Carson just sits there staring at me. I knew these dudes were creeps. Trying to traffic me into LGBTQ prostitution. They saw I was a vulnerable young male, suicidal and all alone, and followed me up here. I have to sneak out before it's too late.

I get up, "excuse me. I have to go to the bathroom."

Delmont grabs me "where do you think you're going boy?"

I quickly try to run but trip on the tablecloth. Delmont says harshly "I got my eyes on you."

The waitress comes by and Delmont just slips a hundred-dollar bill into her pants and pats her on the ass. He grabs me from behind the back as we head out to the car, driving off into the night.

On the drive they're silent. Trying not to let me in on their plans for me. I have come to terms with death but what could await me could be far worse.

We pull over in front of the motel which has a broken neon sign that buzzes where Delmont greets a group of bikers in the parking lot. So, these guys are going to purchase me?

Delmont takes out a couple hundred-dollar bills and the biker

hands him a bag of cocaine. Close call.

We head back to the motel room, a suite. Carson throws me a

beer as if everything's all right. The two laugh as I clumsily

drop it. Then Carson opens the briefcase he was carrying from

the car. I've never seen so many hundred-dollar bills. These

guys are some big-time kingpins.

They go on to snort coke out of the hundred-dollar bills and I

head to the bedroom. I'm way too nervous to sleep. Should I

try to escape? There's a small window but I can't fit through

it.

I just sit there on the bed for the next couple of hours. It was a

big mistake to try to off myself. If I make it out of here alive, I

can make things work.

Delmont comes in and says: "you're sleeping on the sofa". He

slams the door shut once I leave.

I lay down on the old sofa with broken springs that pierce my

back. Looking up into the dark, I can hear them joking around.

Trying to decipher if their muffled voices are talking about me. After another two hours of lying on my back, I finally doze off.

As I doze off, I feel a sense of falling. Then I'm startled to find big fat Delmont lying there naked next to me. He puts his arm tightly around me and then starts licking out my ear, whispering "you're mine little bitch."

Then he grabs my hand, trying to place it on his crotch, but luckily his fat belly gets in the way. I look up at a mirror on the ceiling, but instead of myself, I see a beautiful naked Natalie Bloom being caressed by fat Delmont. I close my eyes and feel Delmont's fat smelly body fade away.

Chapter 16: Fear and Loathing in Reno

I awake to find Delmont standing over me in nothing but a banana hammock with one of his hairy testicles hanging out. Just another bad dream but no escape.

Delmont looks me over, smirks, and then heads back to the bedroom. Now's your chance. I rush to open the door. It's nice out. Just fresh warm dry, pine scented air. Looking out over the parking lot and majestic ponderosa pines, there's even a deer grazing in the woods.

Delmont comes outside, "go fetch us some coffee boy."

I head over to the front desk and get some coffee. It's fresh, not the usual, stale motel coffee. I quickly gulp down the coffee and then bring two cups for them. They ignore me, finish their coffee, and go on discussing business.

As I'm about to get in the shower, I notice one of them has left a brown stain on the only remaining towel. I shower anyways, and with no clean towel I put on my clothes over my wet body.

I head back outside to dry off in the sun. Strangely I don't feel the urge to run. Maybe it's Stockholm Syndrome, or I'm just feeling weak from being out of Klonopin but it's not that bad here. A chance for the adventure that I so deeply desired. Material for a novel I could write to become a number one bestseller and catapult my career as a journalist.

I help them load the truck with suitcases of cash and we head off to Reno to meet with the investor. Perhaps Blackstone staged all this to bring me back to him and help me be his media spokesman. Aren't there some ethical violations about presidential candidates running media outlets?

The drive on the highway passes some magnificent rugged terrain of golden hills and oak woodlands, much like the scenery near my old home around Mount Diablo.

Looking out over a lake from the bridge gets me excited about seeing Tahoe from the car. I should ask them to stop once we get there but I'm a little nervous to ask them for a favor. I try to roll down the window for some air but it's locked.

A few more hours driving through the scenic Sierra Foothills then back up into the forest towards Tahoe. As we drive up alongside Tahoe, I'm too nervous to interrupt them to ask to pull over to check out the Lake. I'll just have to be content enjoying the view from the car.

We're in Nevada now. There's a sign that must be animated neon for the Blackstone Tahoe Resort in Stateline. It's a midrise structure with an alpine chalet theme. I'd love to stop and check it out. Maybe on the way back.

The guys go on about some sex-worker they double teamed, and I anxiously stay silent appalled by their behavior.

We drive away from the lake alongside a massive gorge. I peek back and can see Lake Tahoe below from up in the mountains. There are even some smaller lakes further up into the mountains. I don't think I've ever been on such as spectacular drive.

The mountain terrain becomes more barren and out beyond us is a great desert valley. We'll be in Reno in no time. Delmont says, "we got to stop in Carson City to gamble and take a wiz."

Carson says "Carson? That town's got my name on it."

Delmont replies sarcastically "it sure does."

Carson City has some nice Old West style casinos with cool neon, but unfortunately, it's day time. I recognize Cactus Jack's marquee from my book on historic Nevada. We pull over into a parking lot and I help carry one of their suitcases with hundreds.

Heading into the Carson Nugget, I can't decide which casino has a cooler neon marquee. They get some shots at the bar and I head off to check out the casino. There's just something alluring about the atmosphere of a vintage casino, even the smell of cigarettes and cheap perfume. And it will be fun watching these drunk morons gamble away hundreds of dollars.

The 80s power ballad, "When You Close Your Eyes" by Night Ranger plays alongside the sound of slots. Looking at all the desperate older working class gamblers, I wonder if those oldcels still hold onto their lost dreams of their high school sweethearts as they gamble away their life savings.

After they blow a couple hundred on the slots, we head off, stopping for lunch at some taco bar. Next stop Reno. After a short drive through the desert we reach the exurbs. I've never actually been to Reno but it must have tons of cool neon. Can't wait to walk around here at night.

We stop at our motel to check in. With all that money we should stay somewhere nicer but Delmont insists on only paying with cash and probably uses a fake ID. A little shady but he's treating me so I shouldn't complain.

We stop by some vintage clothing store and Delmont purchases me a beige leisure suit so I'll have something nice to wear when we're out on the town. Too bad I don't have

Blackstone's aviators on me, then I'd really look like a high roller. Right in time for sunset we head Downtown.

Downtown's not quite what I expected; some cool neon but nothing like Fremont Street in Vegas. There are some brand new casinos that don't even have neon and I notice that the cool 70's era neon marquee for the Virginian has been taken down for renovation. Disappointed by the lack of neon, I look up and see something that makes me ecstatic. It's an animated neon billboard for the new Blackstone Casino. It's great that he's bringing back an old artform rather than using those LED screens.

Delmont says: "we need someone who can be the next young pro-Blackstone pundit."

I knew Blackstone had called for me. No reason for me to suspect the worst. This is the turning point in my life. My time to ascend. Given up, on the verge of suicide, and now I'll achieve money and status doing what I love.

Reading my mind Delmont suggests we head to the Blackstone for drinks. The Blackstone Casino is a French themed high-rise structure of black glass with gold and purple neon. In the front is a giant animated gold neon marquee, on the side of the tower is a giant animated gold bulb sign shaped like a French Rococo clock, and on the top are the words Blackstone in glittering bulb signage. The interior is a large atrium designed to look like a Parisian hotel or department store. We walk over to the casino floor and over to the bar.

I ask "are we going to gamble?"

Delmont responds, "No, we have a very important client to meet," and I wonder if it's Blackstone.

Delmont offers me some drinks on his tab. They get shots of bourbon and I get a glass of Champaign. They snicker at my drink choice.

Delmont says "you better not disappoint our client," having no idea that I already shared an intimate experience with Blackstone.

After a couple of glasses of Champaign, we head upstairs to

meet our client. The external elevator even has a gilded style

indicator. As the elevator ascends, I look out onto the

magnificent atrium. The exquisite view causing me to almost

forget my predicament.

Chapter 17: VR Blackmail

At the top is the penthouse suite where an attendee escorts us to the waiting room. Perhaps I was delusional to think it was Blackstone. They used him as a rouse to lure me in. Probably to pimp me out to some high roller client for perverse services. At least let it be someone aesthetically pleasing.

Two men in white coats call for me by name and escort me off. I look back and see Delmont and Carson snickering. They take me to what appears to be a small medical room with what looks like some kind of video game in front of a medical examination chair. The man says: "sit down and relax."

He comes back with a syringe and orders me to place my arm down on the rest. Delmont must have sold me for medical experimentation. Considering my mental health history, they're going to experiment some kind of new anti-psychotic drug on me. The man sticks an IV into my arm and I feel sedated. Almost like taking loads of Klonopin. Then he puts goggles on me. I just lay there feeling like I'm floating in the clouds.

Maybe it's some test of my mental stability to work for Blackstone. I shouldn't always assume the worst. Floating down through the clouds I'm at a wealthy residential neighborhood near my home at night. Loud rap music is playing.

"Down on yo knees. Drinking dat pee. Dats how you get with the nigga."

There's a group of popular teens in line for a party at one of the McMansions. How the hell did these creeps know I was here that night? Did they use my online activity to create a complete psychological profile of me? Using the GPS on my phone to track my whereabouts? They're probably the one's following me by helicopter too.

There's my old crush: my former neighbor, Chloe. She notices me staring at her and rushes off into the party. I try to follow her, but a group of popular guys push me to the side. One of them starts making out with a girl, taunting me "you're never going to get to taste this fine pussy."

Rushing off in tears, I shout: "I'll fucking kill you all!"

Knowing exactly what will happen the starry night sky transforms into a computer screen. That night I came home in tears, utterly humiliated, with any self-respect I had flushed down the sewers. It was the first big party of my senior year when the new crop of freshman girls were invited. Every year since I was a freshman, I would watch from the sidelines.

This was my last chance at the kind of high school experience you see in the movies but that night something happened that changed my life for the worse. Up in front of my eyes on the screen is the avatar "True Aristocrat". Yes, the incel forum. I told him to go for it, to take out those fuckers. Yes, murder them. It was all my fault.

True Aristocrat was Noam Metzenbaum who murdered a bunch of teens at a party a week after I messaged him. After that incident I couldn't live with myself, the guilt and fear that it would be traced to my IP address. The helicopters constantly watching over me and psychiatrist diagnosing me with schizophrenia, putting me on all kinds of drugs.

All the frog avatars of the incel forum float away and I hear screaming, "run!" Teens, naked wearing nothing but Venetian style masks running towards me. Followed by another group of headless naked guys. I try to run back but the force of gravity pulls me in. I have to face what I've done.

I hear the faint sound of crying. I recognize that sound. But everyone is gone now. The mansion, deserted, is permeated with an eerie red light. Rushing around trying to find where the crying is coming from. The walls start moving in. I look back and the walls are now completely closed in behind me. Even if I wanted to escape I couldn't.

At the end of the hallway is a door so I enter. As soon as I enter, the walls immediately close in behind me. No turning back now. Trapped here to face justice for my crimes.

Right in front of me, there she is. That girl, I've been searching for. Forming a circle around her are decapitated guys like headless roman statues. Blood everywhere.

I proclaim: "Natalie it's me. I was sent by Roger Blackstone to save you."

Natalie, unresponsive, continues sobbing. I get down to comfort her, but she doesn't notice me. I look around and remember I'm stuck in this rotunda with no doors or windows. It must be like a video game where I can leave once I defeat the monster and save the princess.

Did something just move? There's maggots crawling out of one of the sockets. Gross. I move towards Natalie to get as far away as I can from the headless guys. Are they starting to move towards me?

Startling me, Natalie screams out in a demonic voice "you did this to me Max. This is all your fault." The voice gets louder "you can't leave Max. You are stuck here. For all eternity. The party you never got invited to. Ironic isn't it?"

The voice turns into sadistic laughter. Then the men take off my VR set. Delmont and Carson are there laughing hysterically. They high five each other and Delmont says "we got him good! The simulation worked liked a charm. The boss will be glad to hear about this."

My entire online footprint: all my deepest desires and darkest fears turned into a VR simulation. Journal entries aren't meant to become real. They should just sit in a crate in the attic or stored on a hard drive to eventually becomes obsolete, never to be recovered. After I gain full consciousness, I protest "leave me alone! I want nothing to do with you and your sick games."

Delmont says "look boy. We covered your ass. Made sure the Feds couldn't trace your IP address to the killer. We've got records of your entire internet search history. From now on you do exactly as we say or we'll report you for inciting the killer, leak out your search history to the public, and with the new deep fake technology we'll make it look like you were an accomplice to the killer and send you to prison for life."

I don't even bother to respond. Delmont adds: "your pathetic little face will be on the cover of every single paper as the leader of the incel uprising."

"Tomorrow we're meeting with the investor and you'll take on whatever role he gives you," Delmont explains. I nod in agreement. I knew all along that this was too good to be true.

Waking up the next day, I'm startled, reminded that I'm still stuck in this dire situation. After I'm done drinking coffee, showering, and dressed, Delmont explains that we are meeting Pax Johnston who owns a network of sports stations and wants to branch out into politics. He instructs me that my only job is to be his and Pax's puppet.

The next day we head off to meet at a conference room in a non-descript suburban office space. The security is tight, and we have to go through a checkpoint. Once we get to the office the security escorts us to meet with Pax. Pax's assistant brings in Delmont and Carson and orders me to stay put.

While waiting in the room I head off to the bathroom. I think I'm going to be sick. I sit down on the toilet and can hear some chatting through the vent: "There's a lot of money to be made in celibacy." It's a guy with a Texan accent. Must be Pax.

Delmont says: "I really don't get kids these days. Back in my day we were always getting laid. We actually knew how to have fun. Must be the soy diets and video games."

Pax says: "young men today are fucking pussies. They'll shit their pants just with the site of a hot chick."

Delmont says: "I brought you your boy but I still don't know about this whole incel thing. Even the biggest dweebs always looked up to rock stars and athletes, the guys who kicked ass and got the ladies wet. Now not getting pussy makes you a superhero?"

Pax says: "this is the very essence of Blackstone's campaign. It's always been that men strived, worked hard, and improved themselves, dreaming of a mansion, yacht, and nice piece of ass. But more and more disenfranchised young men view the American dream as unattainable. Posters on the incel forums think all the jobs are going to be automated, chicks only want Chads until they're 40, and only ugly people are breeding so why even bother when with VR you can now live in your own fantasy world. This is where Blackstone comes in. He's telling young men that they don't have to work hard for shit. That all they have to do is vote for him, and he'll make the society they dream of living in into a reality. Robots will do all the work, rent will be cheap with the new building boom, and then he'll force the rich into becoming a baby making factory, and eventually with artificial wombs to breed an endless supply of hot chicks. It's what nerds call automated luxury communism, except with looks-based eugenics and incels are convinced they'll be the new autistic aristocracy. But it's not just the losers. Now all the cool kids think they're being edgy and ironic by supporting Blackstone. There's even Hipster fags dressing up like that killer Noam and reading from his manifesto at poetry readings. Whether Blackstone wins or not we need to profit off this untapped market. The way to do it is to get ahead of the curve in the VR-Entertainment space. That's what all this is about."

Pax explains that Meschel's production company recently purchased a small, Las Vegas based VR-headset company in a multi-million-dollar deal and redubbed it "Meschel Vision". The company—which originally called their product the "COOMTOOB"—had previously been focused on creating VR-pornography and were currently embroiled in multiple lawsuits accusing their productions of depicting underage girls. But the degree of realism they'd achieved had piqued Meschel's interest enough for him to make the acquisition.

"So where does Max come into this?" Delmont asks.

Pax says: "Meschel's guys used this algorithm, along with a new spyware software to create psychological profiles by screening the search histories of the posters on the incel forums. "Max's Aesthetic World" is a sort of pilot program. If we can prove there's an audience for this kind of nonsense, we'll release the second season through the Meschel Vision VR format, where audiences will have the opportunity to interact and soon, when the technology catches up to Meschel's vision, create their own "aesthetic worlds" to inhabit. We know the audience is there, and when we finally hit the VR dimension of the show, the Meschel Vision 3000 will be the hottest selling item of the year. Max fits all the criteria of what we're looking for to be our guinea pig, and due to his sketchy browsing history, he has to do whatever we say no matter how humiliating, or offensive. Not to mention the surveillance of his meeting with Blackstone."

My anxiety levels rise to an all-time high. I have no other choice but to give them my all-time acting performance. I have to act cool for once. I head back to the waiting room and there's Pax.

I was expecting some older fat White guy with a cigar, but Pax is around 40, a muscular, light skinned African American man with a tightly fit black shirt, shaved head, and goatee.

Pax shakes my hand hard and invites me into his office. He mentions he's a former NFL player.

Pax says: "we're gonna make you a star. Tomorrow we're flying you on a private jet to meet Ari Meschel in LA. You'll stay at a five star hotel and have access to all the finest young tail. Best of all you'll get your own TV show. All you gotta do is sign this."

I quickly look over the contract. Most of it is incomprehensible legal jargon but towards the bottom I notice it says, "I Max von Mueller, hereby sign over the rights of my personhood to Meschel Pictures."

Pax noticing my hesitation says "Max, we know all about your whacko political views, sexual fetishes, every porn site you've ever visited, all those rants on that forum about how you're a loser who's never even kissed a girl. We know all your worst fears too." I start to panic.

Pax changes his tone to reassurance "but if you play ball with us. No one ever has to know about all that. I told Meschel we could play off your persona as a parody of the losers who support Blackstone. We'll even help you cultivate your offscreen persona as the Woke Chad."

I don't trust him, but do I even have a choice? I take a deep breath in and sign the contract.

Pax says "that's a good boy. Now hold on a second." Pax starts grunting and puts his hand down as if he's skull fucking someone under the desk. He shouts, "now get the hell out faggots!"

I look back and Pax is having an orgasm. You know even if my reputation is ruined at least I get to live the highlife for once. Yeah, screw all that idealistic shit. It's all about money, fame, pussy, and just saying the right things. Just Hollywoodmaxx and the world is yours.

The next day we head off to the airport. I've never flown on a private jet before. I look out at the jet with the rugged desert mountains as the backdrop. I'm a bit anxious about flying, and to make things worse, I'm basically a captive. After we take off, Delmont puts his arm around me and whispers in my ear "you're ours bitch."

Down below I can see the desert, mountains, and a lake. Not Tahoe, but probably some desert lake. Reno just looks like a giant grey blob of sprawl, but it probably looks cool at night when it's all lit up. We quickly fly over Tahoe. Too bad I didn't get a chance to go but it looks amazing from the air. I had no idea how massive it was. Amazing how quickly we pass the Sierras. Would have loved to see the mountains from the air.

I look down and admire the quilt-like patchwork of the Central Valley farmland. I have an entire collection of aerial photography books from SF to Tahoe to Vegas. I should make my own now that I'm a star. The plane drops from turbulence and I feel a bit funny in my stomach. The plane starts shaking. Delmont shouts "Yeehaw!" The turbulence gets so bad that the oxygen masks come down. I try to breath in but can't get anything. Hyperventilating until I pass out.

Chapter 18: Vapor City

"Wake up boy." It's Delmont. He informs me we've arrived in LA.

I get off the plane where a Blackstone is awaiting us. We've landed at the Van Nuys Airport.

Once we've passed the Santa Monica Mountains on the freeway, I can see the vast LA basin sprawling as far as the eye can see. With all the new Blackstone proposals I've read about I'm hoping the skyline has grown exponentially since the last time I visited.

We get off the interchange at Wilshire Blvd and pass all the luxury high-rises. The Blackstone drops us off in front of the Blackstone Beverly Plaza Hotel right in the heart of Beverly Hills, off Rodeo Drive. The Art Deco inspired hotel must be 50 stories tall with black glass and gilding along with some other new structures towering over Beverly Hills. I knew Blackstone had lived up to his promises and that the local

NIMBYs must be having heart attacks. We enter the atrium which is one of the most spectacular I've seen. There's even a pool with an indoor tropical garden. I very much want to run off to explore Beverly Hills, but Delmont says that we have business to take care of.

We get onto an external glass elevator. Delmont warns me that if I so much as leave his sight, he will release a webcam shot of me masturbating.

We get off on the level where Meschel has his suite. A hotel suite as an office? A perfect place to take advantage of naïve aspiring actresses. I notice it's not so much part of the hotel but rather a skybridge that connects to a tower where Meschel has an office.

There's an advertisement for the new Blackstone Rodeo Towers development which includes a series of high-rise hotel and residential complexes, and an expanded Rodeo Collection shopping center, all connected by skybridges. Looking out at the view I can see that the area surrounding us is coming together as a more cohesive urban experience.

After waiting an hour, Meschel's assistant says he's busy casting an actress. I feel pity for the Ficus tree. Delmont tells me we're going to Meschel's party tomorrow night but until then I'm not to leave my room. My room is a really cool suite on the 24th floor. I've never stayed somewhere this exquisite nor had an entire room all to myself.

Later at night, daydreaming in my room about the world outside, I'm startled by a knock on the door. I ignore it but this person keeps knocking persistently with this girly voice asking: "let me in." I look through the peephole and see a smoking hot girl a couple years younger than me.

I open up and there she is: exquisite fashion, luscious dark brown hair, cute but smug face, curvy with some nice cleavage. I put out my hands anxiously, "I'm Max, Max von Mueller."

The girl replies "hi, I'm Sarah," and starts rubbing her chest

up against me. I've never had a girl get this intimate with me

and don't know how to respond.

Nervous about her taking things further I suggest "I could use

some fresh air. Let's go for a walk."

She turns to me "I know you like architecture. I want to take

you somewhere special."

Used to being totally invisible, I forgot that I will be the star

with my aesthetic visions broadcast to the masses.

We get on the elevator and get off on the 3rd floor which is a

shopping arcade. She drags me off like a doll onto the

skybridge that connects the hotel to the Rodeo Collection,

originally built in the 80s. I could explore this network of

skybridges all night and the Rodeo Collection is magnificent

too. There are a series of ivy covered brick towers

interconnected by glass tube and brick skybridges, slabs of

white marble, surrounding an open air atrium which has

verdant ferns, waterfalls, and even external glass tube

elevators, illuminated by eerie light and the echoes of synthwave. A futuristic take on an ancient city.

I look up and see the Blackstone looming over us. It's as if Blackstone has been watching over me this entire time and created all this magnificent architecture just for me to explore. But architecture isn't the only exquisite beauty here. Sarah grabs my hand and places it on her breast. I back away to avoid an erection.

She notices me blush and giggles, "I see you could use some experience. My daddy's party is tomorrow night." Her dad is the infamous Ari Meschel? How can such a vile beast like Meschel produce such a gorgeous specimen?

Overwhelmed by the thought of actually getting intimate with her I walk away, towards the waterfall to come back to my senses. That's her. That girl. Yes, its Natalie Bloom dressed in a pink kimono, walking along the other side of the atrium. I run over towards her, but noticing me she runs off, getting onto the external glass elevator. I have to find her this time. But there's Sarah.

"I've been looking for you," Sarah says. She leans in to give me a kiss but I back away again.

Looking offended, she says: "I knew you were gay." Then her expression changes to a more mischievous look: "but my friends and I can change that tomorrow night."

"No, that's not it," I respond. "I have to go to the restroom. I'll be right back."

Losing track of Natalie, I quickly get on the next elevator, but I totally forgot to check which level she got off on.

After pushing a random button, I walk down a long corridor which ends at a rotunda with a lion head fountain. Part of the shopping arcade, but all the stores are closed. No sign of Natalie but this would have been the perfect romantic spot to meet her. I should head back before Delmont finds out, but first I've got to find Sarah and take her back to my suite.

Remember Max, you're the star. You can get any girl in this town so why obsess with just one?

Chapter 19: Emma the Nature Girl

As soon as I wake up, a woman in a French maid's outfit brings me coffee, fresh squeezed orange juice, and scones with cream. She adds that all room service will be put on Meschel's tab.

I just got a text from Delmont:

"We have a party at Meschel's tonight but until then you are not to leave the hotel."

I wanted to go sightseeing, but the Blackstone is its own self-contained city with so much to do.

I've got lots of texts and missed calls from my parents worried sick about me. I was too overwhelmed to even think of them. I feel terribly selfish. Perhaps part of me wanted to make them suffer for dragging me off to Modesto to rot. And they haven't even found out about my show. I lie and tell them that I went on a camping trip to Yosemite with an old friend from high school and will be back next week. My mom is upset that I didn't tell her I was leaving but is glad to hear from me. She

adds that the cops found my dad's car left up in the mountains

and that he had to go up there to retrieve it. I apologize but

don't know how to explain that situation. I'll give her a call

later. I turn on the TV to check up on the latest news with

Blackstone. Oh great there's been another incel massacre. I

really don't want to be associated with this madness.

"Breaking news. A bomb was detonated at Lockden University

in Pennsylvania, leaving 23 casualties including the bomber

Tobias Maxwell Sharpe. Sharpe detonated the bomb inside a

paper mâché dragon, the school's mascot, at the school's

Dragon Day parade. Sharpe had expressed sentiment similar to

the incels about being rejected by women and the popular

crowd and later fell under the sway of Professor Thomas J.

Wallingford: a secret fascist who is rumored to have fled to

Russia. Wallingford also seems to have had covert, executive

involvement in Pennsylvania for Blackstone and is under

investigating for allegedly negotiating a deal between Russia

and the Blackstone campaign, promising access to US

intelligence in exchange for Blackstone visas for Russian women." The newscaster adds "this horrible tragedy occurred right before the premier of Ari Meschel's new show Max's Aesthetic World which capitalizes upon the incel phenomenon, a desperate attempt to revive his floundering career after Meschel's #MeToo incident."

"I'm joined here with Democratic Presidential Nominee Dave Cohen-Rodriguez to discuss incels and the threat that bigotry and misogyny pose to society. What are your thoughts on this disturbing trend?"

Cohen-Rodriguez responds "this is not an issue to make light of. My opponent Roger Blackstone views the incels as a voting block to pander to, as if we can just buy them off with a guaranteed income and state-funded vouchers for sex workers, dismissing their reprehensible bigotry as just a scarcity mindset. I won't negotiate with those who feel that just because they were born a cis White male they're entitled to other people's bodies and if they're denied that privilege they go out and murder innocent people. Young White men need to realize that we are in a global economy and that they must compete on an even playing field with the rest of the world, including women and people of color. Once I'm elected I will shut this all down. Create a database using facial recognition to track incels, sexual predators, misogynists, racists, and fascists. Monitor all their online activity with a biometric ID, criminalize anonymous postings, pressure social media networks and financial services to de-platform them, and notify all their potential employers and the communities they live in. And I'd also use AI to crack down on and criminalize visual sexual harassment directed at women and adolescents."

What is he talking about? That the elites owe nothing to the youth of this nation. What rightwing assholes have always said. He's the real fascist, not Blackstone. Regardless, I've got to certify my Woke credentials in case he does get elected. Make it clear to the public that I don't endorse any of this. The Woke crowd used to like Meschel but they've turned against him for abusing his White male privilege and they'll turn against me just for being affiliated with this.

I get showered, dressed, and head down to the lobby. While admiring the atrium, I feel a tap on my back. A women introduces herself, "I'm Melissa, Meschel's publicist. I've been looking for you. We need to start cultivating your Woke Chad image. We've started you an Instagram, a Bumble, and gym membership at Equinox, plus we've even arranged for you to get a manbun hair extension at the salon. We've also gotten you tickets for a Chainsmokers, DCR fundraiser, concert. After I thank her and get the info for the appointment, I pace around the lobby basking in my newfound status.

I need to do some actual charity work to prove to the public that I'm not a poser. In the lobby I notice a group of Japanese tourists posing for selfies with a cute blonde girl. I recognize her now. Yes, Emma van Lingen, "Emma the Nature Girl", in her signature khaki safari outfit and blonde Dutch braid pigtails. She's a teen girl from South Africa who hosts a TV show, traveling all over the world exploring wildlife. I've had a major crush on her ever since last summer when I came to see her give a demonstration on exotic wildlife at a park in Danville. I came up with this whole environmental presentation to show her but I was too nervous to even ask for her autograph because most of the people at the event were young kids. Now is my chance, remembering that I get to interact with so many cute girls on the show.

"Hi Emma. It's nice to meet you. I'm Max."

Emma smiles, "can't wait for the show, and Blackstone is really cool too."

Wanting to brag I mention "I hung out with Blackstone at his mansion."

Emma says "that's really cool. I'm doing a photoshoot promo for his new resort near San Francisco."

I ask: "are you here to promote the show?"

"I'm actually doing a promo for my own show," she says.

"Great, I'm going to Meschel's party tonight…are you, ah, going to be, going to go?" I awkwardly ask.

She giggles "yeah, I'll see you there. My friend and I are going to the pool this afternoon if you want to join us."

"Sure" I say.

I'm too anxious to think of anything else to ask her so I head off and say: "I'll see you at the pool."

I can't believe such a beautiful girl actually wants to hang out with me and I hope her friend is cute too. I get on the external glass elevator and get off on the level where the arcade is. I was given an app with Blackstone credits to use at the hotel. First, I check out the boutique and purchase a swimsuit for the pool. I have an hour before my appointment at the salon so I'll explore the arcade.

The shopping arcade overlaps the skybridges connecting the towers and has various themes, including a late 19th Century European shopping arcade with glass vaulted ceilings and another section along the lines of the Retro-Futuristic Rodeo Collection with brick and glass where I ended up last night. Blackstone has also proposed an arcade like this that would connect the Blackstone in San Francisco with skybridges to Yerba Buena Gardens and the SF Shopping Centre after the underground segment is completed. But architecture is for nerds. Think of something a Chad would like.

I know. I'll hit the gym later. Maybe that will boost my confidence for Emma. I check in at the salon. Just having everyone at this high end salon fuss over me elevates my sense of status.

I walk out feeling like a million bucks with my new manbun. Strolling around the arcade like a Chad. I see some attractive Asian women and give off my cockiest grin. But they just continue texting while holding onto their shopping bags. You've got to work out first. Build up your T-levels. Just gymaxx.

I head over to the gym which is conveniently located next to the pool. The weight room is packed with handsome, snotty jocks a few years younger than me. On the incel forums, these types of rich asshole jocks are referred to as Chads because of

Noam's manifesto. It feels like being in high school again. And these guys are much more privileged and better looking than even the jocks at my old school. I wonder if they're extras for the show or are their schools paying for them to stay here while people of color sleep on the streets?

I look over their jerseys, Chadsworth Alamo, Chadsworth Woodside, Chadsworth Marin, Chadsworth Carmel, Chadsworth Montecito, Chadsworth Beverly, Chadsworth Palisades, Chadsworth Westlake, Chadsworth Newport, Chadsworth Dana Point, and Chadsworth Del Mar. The most exclusive prep schools in all of California, recently purchased by Blackstone, which he'll subsidize with his eugenic school voucher program, leaving no funds left for students of color. Just a bunch of preppy spoiled brats, stupid high school water polo and Lacrosse players. I've got the real edgy look here and could probably get into the trendiest Hipster clubs in LA and date any of their girlfriends.

Not wanting to be too close to them, and having no experience lifting weights, I just go on the treadmill, as I often go jogging and was on the cross-country team in high school. Screw weightlifting. I'm an intellectual, not some gymcel. After about 30 minutes I head over to the locker-room to change.

Oh great, I hear them coming in. Just hurry up and change. But it's too late, as they crowd onto the bench, leaving me little room. I start to panic as they begin to take off their sweaty jerseys. I close my eyes and start hyperventilating. Are they laughing at me? One of them bumps into me, getting his sweat on me, and doesn't even apologize. I open my eyes, noticing their toned sweaty smooth naked bodies. Blackstone's probably using them for his breeding program. Taking their sperm samples to fertilize artificial wombs like some Nazi mad scientist.... And just look at yourself? Your features are decent, good facial bone structure and all, but you're a framecel lanklet, with an average sized dick which looks pathetic in comparison to theirs. They're younger than you but probably have had more erotic experience than you'll ever have. Face it. They'll always mogg you regardless of how much you status and looksmaxx. If you're lucky you'll betabux for one of the foids who blew them all when she's a post wall roastie.

Stop thinking like a fucking incel!

One of them notices me looking him over, "you ok bro?"

I run off to the shower, quickly rinse off, put on my swim trunks and leave, humiliated. Just don't let Emma see you like this. The pool area is indoors with a retro style glass canopy and a tropical garden to walk through. I look around and notice lots of aesthetically pleasing people. Yeah, just handpick the most attractive women of color. Blackstone will let in some hot Asian tourists, some local rich Persian girls who attend Chadsworth Beverly, perhaps a few lighter skinned LatinX girls, and of course blonde Jewish girls but I haven't noticed a single BIPOC. That's exactly what Blackstone wants to do with his immigration policy and then say he's not racist. Meschel did that too with his films before he was called out for not being body positive. And what makes you think you'd benefit from Blackstone's policies? You're not bad looking but you can't compete with those Chads which he'd just breed more of.

Oh great. There's Emma. I'm really nervous talking to her, especially in her designer bikini. And she has a guy with her too. A handsome blond guy with a lightly tanned complexion whom I recognize from the gym. She'd better not have a boyfriend. You've got to get a drink first. You're a celebrity, they won't card you. Calm your nerves before you talk to her.

"Hi, Max," says Emma.

"Oh, Hello," I respond.

Emma giggles,

"This is my friend Jan from South Africa. He's at Chadsworth Alamo as an exchange student."

I shake his hand,

"Oh, cool. That's right near my home and Blackstone's too."

Jan mentions something about being a rugby player in South Africa and is trying out for the Chadsworth La Crosse team. I knew Emma was into Jocks but he seems cool, and hopefully didn't notice my freak out in the locker room.

I suggest "let's go to the hot tub."

Emma says: "sounds great."

Once we get in Emma turns to me, "I'm really excited about the show."

I ask: "so what's your role?"

She says, "Meschel won't tell me. He doesn't tell us anything about an upcoming shoot and then has us improvise."

Trying to sound cocky, I say "he's a genius. You've just got to trust the man."

She giggles then says "but some of the stuff on the show is pretty weird. The guy they're basing the character on sounds like a real creep, but I know it's a parody and just a character you're playing."

My heart sinks knowing she's disgusted with me, but I'm not a slave to my online posting history. I close my eyes and take a deep breath in, imagining that my entire internet search history and online presence has been wiped clean.

I ask: "so how do you like living in South Africa?"

Emma says "It's a really cool country. My family owns a safari preserve and I've been giving tours there since I was a kid, but crime is out of control and there's a really ugly political situation."

I ask "have you thought about moving?"

She says "I really love it there, but I don't know about the future. If Blackstone gets elected most of my friends and their families are going to apply for visas to come to America."

She then shows me Instagram photos on her phone of her with her friends at the safari preserve, all attractive blonde Chads and Stacies. The girls are gorgeous but why doesn't she have any friends of color?

"Blackstone is cool." I say.

Emma and Jan nod in agreement and then they go on about her work rescuing Sea Turtles in Costa Rica and I feel a bit left out. Just try to think of something ecofriendly to butt in, about how I once helped with a cleanup of trash along the Bay but that sounds pathetic in comparison. Emma playfully ducks under the water, then spits out some water on Jan's chest, giggling. I knew it. They are a couple. Forget about her. You can hook up with Sarah Meschel at the party tonight.

Emma then says she has to go to her room to respond to emails, but she'll see me at Meschel's party.

As she gets out of the hot tub, I get excited looking at all her smooth bare skin, her legs and perfect ass, and can't imagine a girl this hot even giving me the time of day.

Chapter 20: Meschel's Party

I get a text from Meschel's wardrobe specialist who has selected an outfit for me to wear tonight, a blazer and Buddhist medallion necklace that goes perfect with my manbun.

After I'm ready, I meet up with Delmont in the lobby and we head out to the loading zone where a Blackstone auto is waiting to take us up to Meschel's place in the Hollywood Hills.

Maybe losing my virginity to Sarah Meschel will help me stop being such as pussy. I'm already hard just thinking about it. From Culver City we drive up La Cienega. We pass by the Beverly Experience, formally the Beverly Center, which Blackstone has renovated with exterior tube escalators and animated neon displays to pay homage to the original 80s aesthetic. It's also connected by skybridges to a new skyscraper complex across the street. Then up to the Sunset Strip past the Art Deco Sunset Tower hotel and French themed

Chateau Marmont. Blackstone has sponsored some neon initiative for the Sunset Strip which I'm excited to see.

Amongst the neon there's some advertisement for my show, Max's Aesthetic World, which is named after my blog. The fact that it's an LED screen and not animated neon makes me suspect there's some shallow corporate interest behind it.

We turn off Sunset, up Laurel Canyon, and then under the Mount Olympus gate, up into the Hollywood Hills. Meschel's place has a really cool 80s aesthetic. Palm trees, pastel colors, columns, and lots of brick glass. We're dropped off and head out to the backyard where the party is. It's packed with all types of Hollywood bigshots and hot young actresses. I feel anxious starting small talk, so I get a sake and admire the view of the City. The LA skyline is magically lit up at night and has come a long way with the Blackstone in Beverly Hills adding a nice touch. The tropical grotto themed pool is really cool too. This would be such a romantic spot to share with Emma. I should see if she's here.

You're the star here. You've just got to show some confidence. Sleep with Sarah first to build up your confidence with Emma. That's what a Chad would do, even a Woke one. I quickly scarf up some edamame with Siracha and go over and ask the bartender for another sake.

Delmont calls out: "stop being such a loner and come meet Ari Meschel."

There's an overweight middle-aged bald man telling jokes to a group of people. I had no idea he was such a manlet. Like 5'3.

Delmont turns to me, "Max, let me introduce you to Ari Meschel."

Meschel turns around and puts on a big sleazy smile, "Hi Max, how you doing? This is all about you. This is your night. I know you've had a rough few years...."

"You do?" I ask.

Meschel says "we know everything you've posted about your non-existent love life, your most perverse fantasies, and all about your mental health history. But tonight, that can all change. Feel free to hit on any actress here. You're a star, they can't say no. Just stay away from my daughter Sarah. If you so much as glance at her, I'll send you to the seats and have the Chadsworth Lacrosse team use them after practice."

Meschel notices my look of shock and confusion, then says: "I'm just fucking with you Max," and bursts out laughing. Meschel then grabs the arm of a blonde girl out of the crowd. It's Emma.

She awkwardly smiles at me. He then puts his arm around her. Emma looks very uncomfortable and I'm terrified knowing of the #MeToo incidents.

Meschel proclaims: "these South African Shiksas are an untapped resource I tell ya. The girls are all stunning and blonde, and the guys look like they could be Nazi extras for a Spielberg film. These Shiksas keep showing up at my casting calls, desperate for any role to get a green card to get out of that shithole."

I anxiously mumble under my breath, "Emma has a multi-million dollar contract for her own show. She doesn't need you." Meschel ignores me and turns to a man with an Asian wife and says, "stop wasting your time on these flat chested bat eaters when you could have a nice young blonde like this". He starts to rub Emma's chin.

Wanting to prove myself to Emma I say "Emma's a strong independent young woman and she can take care of herself. You're a disgusting old man and why don't you go find someone your own age."

Meschel laughs "oh how cute. I see you have a little fight left in you. If you want to talk about women your own age, let's take a look at all those "art nudes" you have on your browsing history. Why don't we make them public to the entire world as part of Max's aesthetic utopia."

I spasm humiliatingly, and even Emma gives me a weird look.

I protest "Ari, just leave the girl alone."

Meschel reaches up, flicks me right in the face and says "now go get your' dick wet," and points to some bimbo with big, fake, breasts. "That chick there gives the best blowjobs in the industry."

As I walk off ashamed that I failed to prove myself to Emma, I see Sarah Meschel motioning me with her finger to come over. I look back and see Meschel continuing to caress Emma's waist. Emma looks very distressed. I feel like shit for letting Emma down but this could be my chance with Sarah.

Sarah says: "the real party's in my room."

I ask: "let me just finish up my sake?"

Sarah takes my glass and smashes it on the floor, "I got a minibar in my room." She orders the waiter to clean up the broken glass as she puts her heel on his back giggling. Then she grabs me off, not even asking my permission. Into the main atrium and then up the spiral stairway and down a long hallway off to her room. I've never seen a private bedroom this large with high ceilings, pink walls and large brick glass windows. It's not really a bedroom, but rather a suite with a room for sleeping, an entertainment lounge, a large bathroom, and makeup room.

There are two smug girls who look bored sitting on the sofa, even hotter than Sarah. Sarah didn't tell me she brought friends. An orgy? I don't think I can even talk to girls of that caliber without passing out and those cocktail dresses must have cost them a fortune.

Sarah says, "I brought you a guy."

One girl says "eeew." The other says "he's so skinny and looks like a total nerd."

Sarah looks pissed off. Then says: "he's really hot he just needs to loosen up. That's all." The girls sneer at me.

Sarah whispers something in her friend's ears. The girls all start giggling. I wonder what they've got planned for me?

Sarah introduces her friends from Chadsworth Beverly, as Jasmine, a hot Persian girl with luscious wavy dark hair and a light olive complexion, and Zoe who's a pale brunette with cute mousy features.

Sarah says "my daddy said we can be on the show."

Jasmine says "I can't wait to use the seats."

Sarah shushes her and says "not in front of Max."

Zoe adds "and all those hot Chads there too," sneering at me as she says it.

Noticing my solemn expression, Sarah says "don't worry we'll find some use for him tonight."

The girls all giggle and then Sarah orders me to get them a bottle of Champaign from the minibar. I thought I was Sarah's date not her personal butler. I go get a Champaign bottle from the fridge and try to open it without spilling it. I go to the bathroom and open it over Sarah's hot tub. I would love to see the girls naked in there. I pour the girls Champaign in their glasses as they joke around with each other giggling, completely ignoring me. Sarah notices me just awkwardly standing there, silent, watching them.

Zoe and Jasmine scoff at me dismissively and then Sarah turns to me:

"Max, why don't you show these fine ladies what you got."

A now drunk Jasmine starts chanting "strip! strip!"

I unbutton my shirt, then take off my undershirt. The girls laugh mockingly, commenting on my skinny arms.

Finally down to my boxers, Sarah orders me to "take them off."

Terrified, I freeze. "I'm sorry. I just can't."

Jasmine says "afraid to show us your tiny dick? You're pathetic."

Sarah pushes me down onto the sofa and says "I actually thought you were kind of cool but you're just as pathetic as your character. And take off that manbun hair extension. It isn't doing you any good."

I cry out "what do you want from me?"

The girls, ignoring me, jump up on the sofa, still in their dresses. I ask them "aren't you all going to get undressed?"

Sarah giggles mockingly, and the girls all take turns gently kicking me in the face and chest with their high heels. Just the smell of perfume, their feet right near my face, and a whiff from under their skirts is getting me hard.

Jasmine gives me a nasty look.

"This pervert here tried to look up my skirt." Sarah laughs, then teasingly slaps me across the face and says "we didn't give you permission to look up there." Zoe comes over with a blindfold and places it upon my face and says, "you're not worthy to look at us." I'm already hard.

Sarah then orders me to "open wide."

I feel a bunch of lacy panties drop upon my face. Then they proceed to try to stuff their panties into my mouth. They can't fit in my mouth, so the girls just take turns rubbing them all over my face. Smells of sweat, piss, and a hint of arousal.

Sarah then orders me to stick out my tongue and "lick them clean."

I'm reluctant but Jasmine pinches my nose giving me no other choice.

Zoe adds, giggling, "yeah, your fascist Blackstone supporting tongue is only good enough to clean up our filth. Hashtag Resist." The taste is pungent but I'm strangely aroused.

I protest that I have to head back down soon.

Sarah says: "we're not done with you yet."

She backs her large bare ass into my face. "You better get used to this position" she says. "You'll be spending hours in it. Now give it a kiss."

I resist but Sarah presses down hard, rubbing her sweat all over my face. About to suffocate, I kiss her, getting sweat on my lips. She lets out a sigh of pleasure. Next is Zoe. Her skin is so smooth. She giggles, bouncing onto my face as I kiss her ass multiple times. Then Jasmine. She presses her ass right up into me. Very plump with a strong musky scent. I realize that she's a girl of color, even though she's actually quite privileged. I must make amends for all my bigoted thoughts, online postings, and all historic injustices. I stick out my tongue and wiggle it around her sweaty crack. Continuing for about ten seconds. A subtle moan, almost like she's enjoying it. Then slap!

Jasmine says: "I didn't say you could do that."

Sarah says: "he'll get plenty of time to pleasure us like that but that doesn't mean we have to look at his ugly face while he's doing it." Those incels were telling the truth this entire time.

Just as I'm about to leave Sarah says "you're not going anywhere. I got ahold of your search history from my daddy's computer and if you don't want me to leak it out, you're going to be our personal servant."

I spend the next hour massaging and kissing their sweaty feet as they text on their iPhones. Eventually they let me go but I can't find Emma at the party. I'm really terrified Meschel did something to her. When Delmont finds me he says: "boy, you reek of ass. I don't know what you're into but at least you got

laid."

Chapter 21: Piñata Abortion

Today is the first shoot for Max's Aesthetic World. Meschel hasn't informed me about anything and in fact I'm quite nervous knowing the theme of the show and how Meschel gets off on humiliation.

Delmont and I pull up at Meschel's studio in Culver City and admire the high-rise headquarters for Meschel Pictures and all the massive advertisements for the show.

The character for Roger Blackstone has the name Ronald Bluestone as a parody with fake campaign promos. In fact, some are quite offensive with his Beautify America campaign showing him sweeping away masses of freaks and unaesthetically appealing people.

Meschel greets me: "you must be really excited? All those years you spent alone, crying and masturbating yourself to sleep, yeah I've seen all the webcam footage, would you have thought you'd ever be the hottest up and coming TV star?" I smile awkwardly.

He adds "don't hesitate to ask anything of our staff and by anything, I mean anything."

His Asian college aged intern comes over to bring us coffee. Meschel takes a sip and then spits it out right in her face, "I told you. No decaf!"

The girl heads off in tears. I don't want anything to do with someone who exploits others like that, but do I even have a choice?

We head inside to the soundstage to check out the set. I don't see anything other than a green screen.

The technician says it's all virtual so that everything from my dreams and visions will be broadcasted onto TV as well as virtual reality so that the audience can be in Max's world."

The costume team dresses me up in some colorful clothes which look like a Japanese anime clown and put a pink wig on me while the makeup team does my face up to be super girly.

They give me contact lenses which let me see the VR.

I'm ordered on set with no instructions on lines or blocking.

"Action!" Some silly JPOP music comes on and I start skipping around on pink fluffy clouds.

The clouds subside and I'm in some suburban area where each home is just an ugly box with large barren yards. A powerful voice says "that house there is un-aesthetically pleasing. It's owned by some ugly, overweight, old rich asshole, with lots of empty space to spare. Think about all the hot girls little Maxi could have here, rebuild it to be aesthetically pleasing like Maxi's little dollhouse, and be a warrior for aesthetic justice." A man in a frog mask on a unicycle hands me a gas can. The voiced-in audience track chants "burn it down!" I burn the place down.

Walking down the street is a pregnant obese woman whose face looks deformed and already has four mutant looking kids.

I was terrified she would be a person of color with some crude racist joke but at least they made her White to be semi-woke.

Meschel jokes: "she's only good for cleaning my toilet. Totally unfuckable."

I used to think Meschel was a big time progressive before the #MeToo incident. He even gave money to import refugees and house them in some nice, White, middle-class suburbs. But even Blackstone wouldn't sink this low. The frogman gives me a baseball bat and the narrated track instructs me to perform a "Piñata Abortion." I agreed to go along with the show but what if this incites actual violence against innocent people?

Meschel says "don't feel pity for her. She gets fucked whenever she wants while you're still a virgin." I take the bat and look the poor woman right in the eye, trying to think up a good reason to hate her, imagining a future dystopia entirely populated by her descendants, with no one left I find aesthetically pleasing. Meschel says "that's a good boy Max.

She's creating another generation of trash. Taking up space away from hot young ass."

Just get this over with. No. I just can't. I put the bat on the ground.

Meschel shouts: "what a pussy!"

I break down sobbing. Meschel orders me to "just fucking do it already!"

I pick up the bat, slowly walk over to the woman, look her straight in the eye, about to take a swing. Then I stop and again burst out in tears.

Meschel shouts: "cut! Everyone off the set," and runs out in rage.

I overhear the DP say: "we'll just edit it in in post."

I already signed away my personhood to Meschel Pictures and they can now do whatever they please with my image. No, don't look at the woman and her kids again. But she's gone. Must have been a hologram.

Still, I feel guilty for contributing to a culture that devalues and dehumanizes those who don't fit into lookist standards by excluding them from my fantasies. Just focus on cultivating your offscreen persona and make it clear to the public it's a parody mocking bigotry. I run off to the bathroom to cry, visualizing the image of myself carrying out that horrific act on TV. Even if it's simulated. What if my parents see it, all my former teachers, and Lilly too? What will they all think of me? My only friends will be those who just want to latch on to the fame, and then once the show's over I'll have no one. I'll never get hired as a journalist, especially if Cohen-Rodriguez is elected. Blackstone doesn't want to be associated with this either. Everyone in public will know I'm a monster with the new facial recognition app and if I disobey, they'll link that up with my browsing history. And Emma, she's a nice girl but she seems a bit naïve about all this. Once she finds out she'll quit the show, go back to helping animals, and never talk to me again. Just calm yourself down.

I wipe off my tears with paper towels and head back to the soundstage where one of the staff says: "Meschel wants to see you in his office." I'm terrified of the thought of being alone with him.

A security guard escorts me down the hallway. No don't cry again. I hold in my tears and enter the room. I can't even read Meschel's facial expression, whether he's angry or up to another sinister scheme.

Meschel says: "Max, I won't tolerate this level of unprofessionalism from you. I know my directing style is unorthodox but when you signed that contract you agreed to take orders. You understand?" I nod in agreement.

He says: "I could just let you off with a warning, but you'll just keep screwing things up for me." He takes out his phone and says "let me find something cringeworthy from your browsing history with webcam footage of you we can release as part of the show."

I break down sobbing. Meschel laughs "oh, how I love taking the tears and humiliation of incels and political weirdos and turning them into a multi-million dollar profit Hollywood extravaganza."

"Please no. Give me one more chance," I plead.

Meschel says with a sinister expression: "Max, you need to know something about the way the world works. If you're rich, popular, and attractive you can do what you please with those of lesser status. Since you failed that lesson today, you'll have to learn that the hard way."

"I never thought you were a Blackstone supporter?" I ask.

"Not at all," Meschel says, "Blackstone is just exposing the ugliness that is human nature, instead of masking it with the bullshit, pretty lies we're told to keep us in our place."

"What are you talking about?" I ask.

"For instance, Meschel says, think of all the most hot and conceited rich cliques. They never even gave you the time of day and they still think you're trash but now they'll find a more intimate yet degrading use for you."

I start to panic and can tell Meschel is loving it. Meschel creepily looks me over, and slowly picks up his phone to build suspense. He takes the call, "Ivan, how's it going? I need you to come over to my office and escort this boy over to Unit 7. Just drop him off and they'll know what to do with him." Noticing me hyperventilating and shaking in fear, Meschel says "here's a Klonopin, it will help loosen you up."

Chapter 22: Sex Coffin

The security guard shows up, a stern looking muscular Russian man with a shaved head.

I leave with him as Meschel continues to laugh hysterically. We get on an elevator which takes us underground to a maintenance hallway where a golf cart is waiting. Ivan looks at me to get on but doesn't say a word.

We ride down the hallway and make a few turns and then get off. He puts in a code to the door and escorts me in to where another man in a white uniform is waiting for me. Ivan leaves and the man in white instructs me to take a seat in this eerie room with no windows and fluorescent lighting. It feels totally surreal, like a nightmare or what I'd imagine a bad acid trip is like. Another man in white enters the room and orders me to come with him to what looks like a small medical examination room.

He orders me to undress, and then inspects my body. He examines my tongue and mouth, and then runs a scanner over my face. I peak at his phone and realize that the facial scan pulls up what I assume is a dehumanizing caricature of me. Like I'm an item being labeled on an assembly line. I ask the man "what's going on here? But he just smirks and doesn't answer.

Next, I'm taken to a bathroom and ordered to shower. Once I'm done and dried off I run into some fat bald guy with pasty skin and really bad acne scars, not much older than me. He turns to me "this is some fucked up shit here. I never should have posted on that forum."

The man in the white uniform places a bracelet on my arm, orders me to rinse with mouthwash, then sprays my face with a girly smelling substance. He then escorts me down a jail-like corridor totally naked. He pushes open a door and orders me to get into this concrete cubby-like space and to lie down on my back. He then straps my arms and legs in so I can't move. At least there's cushioning so it's relatively comfortable. He checks to see if everything is secure and then closes the door

behind me. I find myself in nothing but darkness. I try to get

up but remember that I'm strapped down. Can't move a limb.

I shout "get me out of here! This isn't funny Meschel!" All

worst case scenarios keep rushing through my head. Maybe I

deserve this for indulging in that kind of stuff. No way.

Remember the lesson of #MeToo. The victim is never to

blame. After waiting alone in the dark for about 15 minutes, I

slowly feel myself ascending upwards, the mechanism

creaking like an old elevator.

I hear something above me starting to move. I look up and

notice a portal open, light pouring in. I hope it's the way out of

this hell.

No......No.....No! A buttocks. Up above. Mocking my low

status. At this moment it hits me what is about to happen.

I hear giggling up above. Like the giggling is coming directly

from the ass, ridiculing my predicament as it slowly descends

upon my face. I'm quickly pushed up, my face tightly

submerged into the sweaty cheeks. Then whoever positions her stubbly slimy pussy right over my mouth. Totally overwhelming my senses of touch, sight, smell, and soon taste. And what makes it even worse is I have no idea who is up above. If she's hot I can survive this ordeal but what if it's like some public restroom where anyone can use it. In Blackstone's world perversions are regulated by high aesthetic standards, but I met the man and he wouldn't approve of this conduct. She positions herself and presses down hard upon me.

Intimidated, I give a few kisses. Then I start, lapping up a slimy fishy mixture of built up stale urine and vaginal secretions. I'm able to tell by her taste and texture, despite the poor hygiene, that she is quite attractive. Perhaps a Chadsworth cheerleader, sweaty after cheer practice. Finally, I feel her contract around my face as she orgasms, letting out the cutest little noises, to the song "Without Me" by Halsey, the favorite of all vapid brats, to the lyrics:

"Tell me how's it feel sittin' up there. Feeling so high but too far away to hold me."

Then the buzzer goes off and I descend back downwards, the portal closing over me. As I lie there alone in the dark with her sticky fishy funk on my lips and face, I remember what Noam wrote in his manifesto, about how if his revolution to establish a new aristocratic imperium, and quest to win over his crush failed he would admit defeat and submit to his oppressors like this, as his aesthetic betters. And Meschel bought the rights to Noam's manifesto right after the trial. There's nothing capitalism doesn't co-opt but I suppose accepting your place in the hierarchy is preferable to being obsolete, masturbating alone to unattainable delusions of grandeur. The man then opens the door, cleans my face, and then sprays me with the girly substance.

While licking out the next pissy cunt I hear some muffled squeaky girly talk, "you know that guy from Meschel's new show? He's like soooo cute!"

I knew the show would raise my social status. She continues "I wish he was under me right now. But yeah, I know. It would be kind of creepy to think about an actual guy in the seat." She even left her tampon in, the string tickling my lips. Luckily there's no blood but still inconsiderate. She giggles and then lets out a high pitched squeal as she orgasms.

After I'm cleaned up and given some time to rest, I think if I survive this ordeal I'm going to become a real man; eat synthetic red meat, lift weights, and get my dick sucked like a Chad." I hear the buzzer and then ascend upwards again. Great another client. My heart races hoping it's someone pleasant.

It's a nicely shaped buttocks. My face presses up against the smooth plump backside which completely engulfs my face. Wait, I recognize that scent, and texture too. It's Jasmine. She presses her full weight upon me. But my face is positioned under her ass making it hard to reach her pussy. I strain my tongue, trying to get to her clit but she tightly clenches her cheeks over my face. Is she trying to tell me something? Not able to reach her pussy, I just lick inside of her sweaty cheeks.

272

Then she parts her cheeks, allowing access to her anus. I get to

work as she gently rides my face with rhythmic motions. I've

never felt this sense of disparity in power and status before.

Intimate for one party, yet totally discreet for the other. The

sense that their personhood totally consumes your

consciousness and senses, yet to them you're just an

accessory. Our relationship with the popular clique, the

attractive, high status, and socially successful. Like we're

there just to give them likes on social media, to kiss their ass.

They unload their waste, which we ingest, the particles of their

superior genes and all the most intimate facets of their life,

secreted on us as the focus of our entire consciousness.

After I'm done I call out to Meschel that I've learned my

lesson and can go now. But the buzzer goes off again

anyways. As for the next round of clients my tongue just goes

into auto pilot, working away on their privileged assholes and

pussies. The muffled sounds of the girls chatting and giggling

with their friends. The feeling of their anatomy upon my face,

their weight pressed upon me, ass sweat, pussy juice, and

remnants of piss drench my face with the rhythm of each orgasm, and the various scents and tastes of arousal and poor hygiene. Some fuck my face hard, some gently gyrate, and some just sit there. I should be almost done by now. I hope Meschel hasn't forgotten about me.

I hear the buzzer again. Oh, that looks like a nice smooth ass. Toned too. She must do squats.

Wait a second. No Fuck! There are two balls dropping down. I've already debased myself, but this is too much. Moving slowly towards me, as if this individual wants to taunt me. I'm now barely an inch from making contact and the stench of sweaty balls is overwhelming.

I hear a cocky voice speaking with his friend: "it's not an act fit for any self-respecting person but hell, there's enough trash out there to keep our assholes licked clean, no real harm done. What else are you going to do if you're born poor, ugly, or autistic."

Probably some cocky, rich Chadsworth jock. And after this ordeal is over he'll make out with some cute innocent Chadsworth cheerleader while you'll be left with the shame of this for the rest of your life. I'm just frozen there with enough distance to prevent contact, but still close enough to be utterly humiliated, and utterly mogged. Then I feel myself about to move up again, my heart beating faster. Just close your eyes and get this over with, imagine it's a girl. Suddenly the buzzer goes off and I descend back downwards. That's a relief.

When I get back down the men in white undue my straps and let me go. They let me shower, rinse out my mouth, spit out all the pubic hairs, and give me some anti-biotic tablets. My tongue is sore and perhaps still sullied with traces of their DNA and microbes. I just feel totally used.

In the waiting room there's Meschel laughing hysterically with an odd-looking young woman, totally naked, with a shaved head, monobrow, flat pig nose and a freakishly long tongue. Meschel says laughing, "Max, I got you good. You almost ate that Chad's ass," then he points to the girl, "that's what this femcel is here for." When she finds out she starts screeching and trying to bite the men who restrain her. I remember reading about femcels on the incel forum but had no idea they were a thing. Whether it's part of the show or not. This is the final stage of capitalism once we stop paying lip service to freedom and equality. I feel sick just thinking about it. Meschel and I get on the golf cart and head back to his office. It must be really late at night and I haven't even eaten anything, or at least nothing substantial today.

Meschel lightens up and says: "so Max, what did you learn today?"

I respond in a monotone voice, "that if one is beneath you, you can harm what is most precious to them. And if they're above you, you must place your highest orifice upon their lowest."

Meschel smiles, that's a good boy little Maxi," and pats me on the head. "I got a treat for you," he says. He offers me an apricot tart and sparkling orange juice from the catering and crumbles up the tart, making me eat out of his hand. "Good little foid-licker" he says, patting my head. He looks at me like his little puppy as I eat from his hand. He adds: "I know this was a lot for you but it was a test. You passed and I now know I was right to select you for the role."

Meschel orders me a chauffeured ride back to the Blackstone. I'm glad this ordeal is over but am terrified things could only get worse. What if Meschel has footage of today to further blackmail me into doing something even more degrading?

Once I get back to the Blackstone, I remember I have to look for Emma to see if she's ok. I'm terrified that Meschel or his daughter Sarah have already corrupted her, and I have visuals of her being one of those girls using the seats, arousing, but destroying any chance at romance and a relationship based upon mutual respect.

Chapter 23: Your dreams are copyrighted

When I wake up the next day, I get a text that I have the day off to relax until the next big shoot tomorrow. While taking a stroll at the arcade, I notice Emma in one of the boutiques. She smiles and says hello but I can tell something is off. She asks me how the shoot was yesterday. Then I panic, realizing she's going to see the show. I keep my response very simple. She mentions that she's going to be at the shoot tomorrow. I ask Emma if she wants to have coffee. She says: "I need to talk to you about something in private." We find a quiet spot off to the side of the atrium. I'm really nervous being alone with her.

I ask her: "is everything alright? From the other night?"

She says "that's what I wanted to talk to you about. That Meschel is a real creep."

"I'm so sorry," I say, trying to comfort her.

She says "I left the party with a friend after Meschel started groping me. Then this morning he entered my room in his bathrobe and said not to wash down there for the shoot

tomorrow. I don't even know what he's talking about." I panic

remembering the poor hygiene of the clients of the seats.

I say awkwardly "don't worry, I'll look out for you."

She just smiles and then says she has to go meet with her

agent. I pace around the Blackstone to pass the time. I just

don't feel the same allure, that ethereal aura of when I first

arrived. It's all just a simulation where I'm the avatar of some

other player with no sense of control.

"Uh, I told you to keep the Prada skirt in the bag."

I turn around, noticing a familiar voice. That girl is gorgeous.

Yes, she's one of the girls from the seats, a Chadsworth

student no less, who just got off from a shopping spree on

Rodeo Drive as her entourage carries her shopping bags. I

overhear someone point to her, mentioning that she's the

socialite daughter of a billionaire fashion mogul who's

manufacturing those "your best is only good enough for my

worst" line of panties. I can't believe I shared such an intimate experience with a girl of that stature. Even if she left a sticky smelly mess on my face. I smile at her but she just ignores me, bossing around her help. I go back to my room and check on the news with the election.

DCR is still the frontrunner, with Blackstone going from 4 points to 8 points behind, with concerns that the recent incel massacre, Russia-gate scandal, and the show might harm his campaign. The first episode hasn't aired yet, but there's a promo of me carrying out that unspeakable act next to surveillance footage of me with Blackstone outside his mansion. I feel terrible that I could somehow be responsible for him loosing after that special night we shared. And the Woke media is trying to claim Ari Meschel is a Blackstone supporter, like they don't even get irony. Before #MeToo he attended every Democratic Party fundraiser.

Jackson is way behind, and has basically given up on challenging DCR. He's just being used as controlled opposition to undermine Blackstone for any right leaning voters, trying to prove to conservatives that Blackstone is to the left of DCR while simultaneously smearing him as a fascist, a psychedelic Hitler. There's a news segment about how this election's theme is the future of the American Dream in this impending era of automation with Jackson defending the outdated model of striving for a corporate job and saving up to buy a home in the suburbs which primarily resonates with older voters who were able to make that work. There's even clips of campaign commercials for the candidate's visions for the future.

DCR's depicts a family of color, a South Asian father and African American mother. Their trans child comes home in tears after being bullied for not fitting into a certain aesthetic mold. They show their parents an image of some rich blonde preppy teenagers who look like Chadsworth students. The trans child says: "I want to look like them when I'm older."

Next it shows the parents volunteering for DCR, followed by imagery from the future of successful women of color at a corporate board meeting. The transgendered child of color was evidently able to become a corporate consultant because DCR was elected. Then a quote flashes across the screen: "if we accept inclusivity we can all rise to the top." That doesn't even make any sense. There's always going to be a limited number of slots at the top, but we all deserve a decent life and place in society regardless.

There's even some released footage of DCR speaking at a finance summit where he said that rising working class White male unemployment is ok as long as it opens up jobs for women and people of color. Just in time for the release of his own version of a Basic Income which would be conditional on an intersectionality score calculator and a social credit score based on monitoring online activity for anti-social behavior. I suppose all political systems and societies pick winners and losers: favored groups to thrive and pass on their genes.

This next campaign add is Blackstone's. The opening scene is of a communal pod housing unit for workers who lost their jobs to automation. The captions says "DCR has been elected and we're 5 years into the future". There's a depressed lone White guy in line with lots of menacing looking people of color for his daily serving of some gruel. He then escapes into a VR simulation that shows the world that could have been if he had voted for Blackstone, of futuristic self-contained cities, all kinds of artistic and scientific innovation, and lots of attractive people swimming in lakes. Screw all that Woke bullshit. I think Blackstone actually wants to advance civilization and his policies are much better for my self-interest.

The newscaster mentions that Blackstone is going into overdrive on funding for adds because he fears the show is creating a lot of negative publicity and if it does cause him harm, I'm to blame. I must set things right. Find out a way to make things clear to the public.

The TV is interrupted by lots of loud police sirens. I look out the window and see tons of protestors and a police motorcade down Rodeo Drive. I go downstairs to check out the commotion. The entire lobby is blockaded by the police to keep the protestors from storming the front entrance. There's a large group of anti-Blackstone protesters in front, calling themselves Beverly Hills Antifa, holding signs with the usual woke slogans against racism and lookism, demanding that the show be canceled.

As soon as I step outside one of them notices me from across the blockade, "that's him. That bigot from Blackstone's TV show. Get him! Get that Nazi fuck!" Another yells "I'll fuck up your face for what you did to that woman!" One of them, in a ski mask, sprays some foul smelling liquid but it accidently hits a group of wealthy Middle Eastern tourists who then run off screaming. The masked man blends back into the crowd so the cops can't catch him. Imagine how much more hated I'd be if my browsing history were to be released? A security guard advises me to stay in my room until the situation is under control.

The next day I head back to Meschel's studio in Culver City for the next shoot. When I arrive there are large groups of Chadsworth brats getting off these luxury busses. The girls are all wearing Lululemons which perfectly highlight the shape of their backsides. The same backsides that sat upon my face.

Cheeks perfected by generations of assortative mating. I have flashbacks of the Chadsworth brats' asses from the seats and I try to guess which ass goes with which of the smug faces I see before me now.

One of the girls getting off the bus look familiar. Yes, that's Chloe. My former neighbor. And she transferred to Chadsworth in Alamo no less. It's good that she's still in the area. I'll say hi to her later but don't want to appear too desperate. And the Chads from Newport in their Lacrosse jerseys as well as the Alamo girls in their equestrian uniforms. Yes, they're all going to be extras on this show that I'm the star of.

I wait around sampling the gourmet snacks but am too awkward to make small talk with the cast, and obsessively look around to see if any of them pay attention to me. I look over and see Emma with the Newport Chads surrounding her, flirting with her. I recognize the cocky laugh of that handsome blonde Chadsworth lacrosse player as the guy from the seats. Just everything about his looks and body language exudes privilege. Why would Emma want anything to do with me when she could have a guy like that? I was delusional to think I ever had a shot with a girl like her. You're a celebrity, dammit. Have a little self-respect.

I walk over to some of the Alamo equestrian girls and try to give off my cockiest smile. Play hard to get. They'll come to you. One girl notices me ogling them and gives me a look of disgust. I'm not smooth enough not to get #Metooed. Just stop giving off weird anxious vibes. It's bad enough you're being used to capitalize upon incel culture.

I look for something to drink to calm my nerves, but the DP calls us onto set. One of the staff orders me to come with him. Escorting me down an elevator to the creepy underground network of maintenance hallways. Great, I have to serve those Chadsworth brats in the seats again. We end up heading over to some medical examination type room, but it's a different place than before.

One of the men in white orders me to lie down on a medical recliner, gives me a pill, a sedative, and tells me to stay put for now. About 15 minutes later Meschel arrives. Meschel says "Max, I got a big surprise for you. Hold on a second." Meschel pulls out his phone and starts reading "look you incel pieces of shit. I've used so many of you like that and you know what? You're just an accessory, something I use to feel good." I wrote that on the incel forum one night when I was bored. I created a sock puppet account of a rich popular girl, using the image of Alicia Silverstone from Clueless, looking for incels to exploit. Meschel notices my look of embarrassment and just keeps laughing.

The man in white inserts an IV into my arm. Then I slide back into an MRI. I find myself floating away into a tunnel of pink fluffy clouds. "I think he's asleep now." Meschel?

"With the new technology we can access Max's or anyone's dreams and turn them into a VR simulation that all the actors can partake in. Yes, when he signed over his personhood his subconscious came with the package. That's the only way we can find that blonde Jewish chick he was talking about with

Blackstone."

Chapter 24: The Real Natalie Bloom

How did I end up back in bed? Max, you really need to get your mental health in check. You're losing it man. My vision's still a bit blurry so I can only make out a big blur of pink. Rubbing the sand from my eyes, my surroundings start to take form, realizing I'm in a really high-end hotel suite. Must have had my rooms switched at the Blackstone. This room is even more exquisite than the first. Yes, really exquisite but quite girly. I look out the window to check the view.

All I can see is the sea at sunset. Must be up in a high-rise but this is definitely not the Blackstone in Beverly Hills. Down below is a boardwalk with neon lighting, and an animated bulb sign saying "Vaporwalk." Up on a hill on the other side of the turquoise cove is a tall lighthouse. Like some kind of seaside resort. Or perhaps that Vapor Island resort Blackstone is building inside a dome off the Vegas Strip.

I walk over to the gilded Rococo mirror. "Natalie Bloom?" I scream. "I'm Natalie fucking Bloom!"

The high-pitched screech nearly breaks my eardrums. That Meschel is really fucking with me. Must be a magic mirror. But remember what Blackstone said. That if I find his long lost love he'll turn my life around. Perhaps even forgive me for the show.

I'll have some fun with her first. Then turn her over to Blackstone. Experience what it's like to not just be a girl, but one of the most ultimate status. One who could have any guy at her fingertips. You've just got to treat her body with respect.

But I suppose a little fun won't hurt. I open up my silk robe and run my fingers down. Oh yes, nice firm perky tits. Down my stomach, down to the smooth dark blonde curly pubes. The inner thighs, with the right thickness and smooth skin that would be perfect for cunnilingus. I take my finger, run it around the labia, and then lick my finger. I can tell by her taste that she's quite innocent. Not like those sluts from the seats.

Suddenly a theme song starts playing to the melody of the 80s ballad "Thunder In Your Heart."

"Max was on a journey. To find the girl of his dreams. The perfect young maiden, but she was he, all this time. In an aesthetic utopia. All your dreams can come true, because it's Max's aesthetic world of glory."

Then the chorus,

"She's the girl of your dreams. Whisk her away to paradise. It's the power you feel when you get your first taste of pussy. "

Suddenly I hear "cut! That's a wrap." It's all part of the show. But the girl I saw in my dreams. Was I her all along? All that romantic energy I was looking for was within me this whole time. All my deepest romantic desires overwhelmed me to the point of consuming me that Blackstone wanted to track me down and access my subconscious. And now Meschel too. The DP says cut and Meschel comes out and starts clapping, "bravo, bravo. I knew you could do it Natalie. The next teen starlet, like a young Alicia Silverstone."

Meschel then yells at the crew to get out. I start to panic.

After the crew leaves, Meschel starts ranting "they thought they could take me down with all that #MeToo bullshit. I'm the greatest damn visionary in all of Hollywood and the women love me. Yes, I've given so many young women a chance at stardom."

He takes his hand, cups it around my breast and smacks me right on the ass. I look behind me and notice there's a neon sign reading: "Casting Couch Maxxer."

He thinks this is all one big joke but if I can't escape from him as Max then I'll #MeToo him as Natalie Bloom. Meschel puts his arm around me and whispers in my ear, "you can call me the Schlomomaxxer." Then he opens up his robe, revealing his fat belly and tiny prick buried in a thicket of bush, and starts fondling himself, grunting. I've got to get out now, preserve Natalie's purity for Blackstone, as well as preventing any emotional trauma that could be transferred back to Max.

As I leave Meschel mentions: "we have another shoot after brunch." I hurry down the external glass elevator which overlooks the cove. After I finish up my crepes and mimosa in the lobby, I run into Sarah and her friends. Meschel returns and says "I see you two have met? Let's get this scene." The DP says "Pleasure Seats. Take one."

"Natalie, I got a surprise for you," Sarah says.

"Yeah?" I reply.

You know about the Pleasure Seats?" The moment I hear those words I panic.

Zoe says "you haven't used them? We're heading over there later."

Jasmine says "like multi-orgasmic. One after the other. And the best part is you don't even have to look at them."

"Can you excuse me?" I ask.

I think I'm going to be sick. I rush to the trash bin feeling the urge to vomit. Not being able to throw up, I just try to take in some deep breaths. Meschel turns to the cameraman, "make sure you catch this."

Hearing my heaving sounds, Sarah tells me "you don't need to do that. Don't let guys make you feel self-conscious about your figure. After you use the seats you'll never have to worry about pleasing a guy ever again."

"I just got a text, "Sarah says. "The Newport guys will be here any minute."

"Newport guys?" I respond.

Sarah continues "yeah, the Chads. All the most popular hottest guys from their Lacrosse team are on the island to celebrate a victory." So much for her spiel about not having to please guys.

I tell Sarah "we're the hottest girls here. We can have any guy kiss our asses."

Sarah says "not if Blackstone has his way. When everyone is hot we'll just be one of many. It will completely destroy our entire way of life.

Jasmine mentions "my cousin in Israel likes Blackstone because she's thinks he'll get her a visa to come to LA to model."

Sarah says: "Blackstone only wants blondes like that Emma bitch from South Africa."

I butt in: "I heard he really likes Jewish girls, especially blondes." Sarah and Jasmine give me puzzled looks.

Trying to change the direction of the conversation, I inquire "did Blackstone set up the pleasure seats?"

The DP says "cut! It's Bluestone."

I repeat "is Ronald Bluestone behind the pleasure seats?"

Sarah says "yeah, Bluestone constructed the venue as a way to employ losers who are unemployable due to automation and creepy political views. With the profits from automation we have a lot more disposable income to spend on these luxuries."

I panic remembering she's parroting what I wrote on the incel forum and that a lot of gullible people might associate this exploitation with Blackstone when in reality he wants to use aesthetics to ease extreme disparities in status.

I go back over to the catering to see if I can get another mimosa to calm my nerves.

I see Emma all by herself, sipping a soda. "Hi Emma. What's your role for today's shoot?" I ask.

Emma responds in confusion. Then I remember that I'm not Max. Just act as a fan, tell her how great it is to finally meet her, and what an inspiration she is for young women.

Meschel calls for us to come over to the conference room for a presentation. Once everyone sits down, Meschel announces we have a very special guest speaker for today. Wendy Silverstein from Chadsworth Academy in Greenwich Connecticut. The brave young woman who organized all these oral sex parties in response to Noam's massacre. She recently gave the most inspirational speech at the Resist Rally about the anti-phallic intersectionality of gun control and cunnilingus."

Wendy gets up on stage, a beautiful blonde Jewish girl in a pink pussyhat, and takes the mic:

"Ari, I want to thank you so much for making this happen. It's an honor to work with you. I know some in the media are accusing you of glorifying misogyny but let me say this. We can sell exploitation as woke if those being exploited are unlovable bigots."

Meschel grabs the mic: "thank you Wendy. This will totally get #MeToo off our backs. Show them who the real feminists are and that they're all just a bunch of puritans who hate sex. We don't let bigots and misogynists off easily with some lawsuit. No, we really make them pay for their crimes."

Wendy mentions "there's a new app where, with facial recognition, you can identify any incel and fascist in public and have access to their entire search history. Now that they won't be able to show their faces in public, the only role left for them will be is the seats." The entire audience of Chadsworth girls in pink pussyhats applaud.

Since I'm not Max I don't have to play by Meschel's rules. As I walk up, Meschel looks anxious but Wendy hands me the mic. I say: "yes, it's a parody of class oppression where the youth of the 1% anonymously humiliate and exploit those of lesser status, the poor, socially awkward, and unattractive. And it's a great way to deal with the excess losers of late capitalism. We can even frame it as an act of Nobles Oblige to make them feel like they have some use in the hierarchy."

Meschel, looking annoyed by my speech, grabs the mic back. "Thank you Natalie, and thank all you young women for your work in making all this possible." He bows down awkwardly, smiling, as the audience gets up and heads off for refreshments. Afterwards I notice Emma looks upset about all this. I remember she's now in Max's subconscious and she could find out all of his darkest secrets. Just imagine her using the seats and then getting up and seeing Max's face with a complimentary quote from his posting history. I want to start a conversation with her to convince her to avoid the seats, but Sarah tells me I have to go with them upstairs for my makeover to look my best for the Chads. Zoe and Jasmine do my makeup and select an outfit for me: the sluttiest, most revealing dress they can find. Zoe mentions that the Chads are ready and we hurry back downstairs.

When we get back down to the lobby, the Chads are urinating into the lobby's fountain of Noam gargling piss. I wonder why these guys are so crude coming from such an exclusive prep school?

They turn around. All four blonde guys, stunningly handsome in their preppy Chadsworth Lacrosse jerseys. Sarah introduces me to Zach who is tall. He has a cute but smug face and a mane of golden blonde hair. Zach just puts his arm around me. I've always fantasized about what it would be like to be part of one of those popular couples and now I sort of get why Sarah selfishly doesn't want to share this with the masses.

The other guys pair up with Sarah, Zoe, and Jasmine as we head out to the Vaporwalk. The air smells fragrant, but not like how the beach usually smells, more piped in like inside a

Vegas casino or ride at Disneyland.

Chapter 25: Seats of Privilege

One of the Chads suggests "let's go to the arcade."

Sarah says "I got a better idea. I got us VIP passes to the Pleasure Seats."

The girls all squeal in excitement. There's an animated bulb sign that says "Pleasure Seats" making it look more like an amusement park ride than an exclusive erotic venue. In front of us in queue is my old neighbor Chloe with her friends, also cute blonde girls in preppy equestrian uniforms, licking their whirly pops. They must be extra sweaty down below from horseback riding. One girl says: "when we get back home we're going to Blackstone's Oasis waterpark near our school."

Trying to get more info, I ask "where do you go to school?" One of the girls just looks at us smugly.

Chloe replies "Chadsworth Alamo."

I remember overhearing even the most popular girls from my high school saying those Chadsworth girls were some stuck up bitches. Just try to think of something to say to Chloe. Trying to remember all the girls in the seats and wondering if Chloe was one of them. Sarah, catching me looking her over, says "don't waste your time on these losers" and shows the attendee our passes as we cut in front of the girls. They look so pissed.

We all pass the aesthetic selector facial recognition scan used to keep out any undesirables. Then we enter through a long pink tunnel that causes me to panic, reminding me of the anatomy I stared up into. Everything smells so intensely of perfume. Noticing the guys, the security guard says "wait. No guys allowed!" Sarah shows her our VIP pass and the woman apologizes and escorts us to the VIP lounge. There's a group of stuck-up teen girls leaving.

Sarah mentions they're the top influencers trending on TikTok. They happen to be some of the hottest girls I've ever seen. And then Emma too, rushing out with an upset expression. Meschel already corrupted her. She was probably a virgin too. Screw it. I'm using the seats. You'll experience pleasures you couldn't even dream of as Max. The higher your status the more intense your orgasm at the expense of those of lesser status. Just don't think of them as human, they're just an accessory there for you to enjoy.

A staff member says we need to watch a safety video but the girls just ignore her. Before we enter the lounge there's a changing room. I suggest we all wash down there to show some consideration for the staff, but the girls scoff. They get undressed, revealing their nicely shaped bushes and all around hot bodies. They then put on some fancy lacey robes. The guys just keep on their sports jerseys. The VIP lounge is all girly with rose colored puffy walls, chandeliers, comfy sofas, and a minibar.

One of the Chads says: "I heard one of the girls back at Newport talking about this place." Another Chad asks Sarah "so why are the seats for girls only? Is there like a vibrator attached to the seat?"

Sarah explains "you sit down like you're on the toilet and it gives you oral pleasure."

He responds "so I stick my dick in?" Sarah is confused how to respond.

Jasmine suggests: "you sit down and it pleasures your ass."

"My personal favorite," Jasmine adds.

Zach says "one of my bros got that done by some drunk girl at a party and he said it feels even better than head."

Zoe mentions they also have a masseuse who will rub your feet while you're getting eaten. We share a bottle of champagne and then it's time for the Pleasure Seats. One of the Chads suggests they also get head from the girls.

Sarah says "yeah, like we don't do that."

Jasmine says "yeah, we're not sluts."

The three girls, agreeing to get their asses pleasured, head off to the stalls leaving me alone with the Chads. The Chads take off their jersey's revealing their toned chests. Zach takes an ice cube and rubs it around his nipples and teases me to lick it.

I keep forgetting I'm a girl now and I can't fall for him

because I have to keep Natalie pure.

I politely reply: "no thank you."

Zach looking annoyed, grabs me and pulls me off to the

pleasure seats. The stall is a pink puffy room about the size of

a small bathroom with a comfy pink chair that opens like a

toilet. There's a warning sign that says "Please do not urinate

in the seat. Toilets are down the hall." I wonder if any of the

girls disobey that warning?

To the side is the control panel and there's also a video screen

and VR set to use while using the seat. A hologram promo

says: "you can simulate that your favorite actor is going down

on you on a tropical beach." Zach opens up the lid, pulls down

his shorts and boxers, and sits down on the seat, looking over

the control panel. I try to avoid making eye contact with his

crotch. He says: "this will put you in the mood."

He turns on the video and it's the new music video by the rapper "DJ Suck it Bitch." His number one hit was "Drink Da Pee."

In the video the rapper's getting a blowjob from a pretty upper class African American woman, the kind that even Blackstone would hand out a visa to, while her boyfriend who looks like Carlton from the Fresh Prince of Bel Air is licking out his ass. It's hard to imagine coordinating the choreography of dancing and rapping while engaging in those acts with the woman in front and the guy down on his knees from behind.

The lyrics go "Get down bitch: Down on yo knees! Suck muh dick. Gonna make yo boyfriend muh bitch. He's gonna lick muh crack while you suck muh dick."

Zach orders me, "on your knees."

I reluctantly get down, keeping eye contact with his chest. Zach puts his hand on my head causing me to accidently stare at his big dick. I try to back away, but he pushes my head down. Resisting, my face lands on his stomach. I can hear the sound of the coffin creaking up. Wow, his stomach is nice and

toned. I start rubbing his sweaty toned chest, massaging every

muscle as my face is buried in his stomach. He moans as he

pushes my head further down, pleading for me to suck his

dick. My chin brushes against his dick and pubes.

I can't go through with this since I must save Natalie's purity.

Instead, I start kissing him all over his stomach and chest, then

start using a little tongue. Tastes salty from his sweat but it

turns him on. Get him to cum so he won't rape you. He then

pushes my head down hard. His dick right in my face.

"What are you waiting for?" He says.

I start licking out his sweaty inner thighs, his balls now

brushing up against my face. I'm now able to sense the

presence of a person in the seat. Visuals hitting me of what

that person is going through. Can they even see up into this

world of pure luxury? The ultimate disparities in privilege and

culmination of class oppression. The aesthetic based hierarchy

only adds a more cruel dimension to those dynamics. I can

hear the muffled sounds of slurping and gasps for air as Zach sits there with a ticklish expression.

"Oh fuck!" Zach moans in ecstasy. I move aside, as his dick starts to contract, shooting massive ropes of cum across the room, one after the other. When Zach gets up, I catch a glimpse of his perfect toned ass. He then pulls up his pants and leaves with little interest in me.

I lock the door, figuring out what to do. I avoided looking at the face in the seat but I'm curious to see who it is.

I recognize him. Yes, it's that Indian guy from the incel forum. Yes, Currycel500. I recognize his face from when members would post their images and other posters would comment on their facial flaws. Gross he smells like a dirty jock strap. A compulsive urge to spit on his face. Giving me tingles just watching him there in this helpless position. I look over the control panel and see the button for cleaning. The cover goes over his face and after a few minutes he reemerges smelling all fresh and perfumy.

I have all this erotic energy built up from the whole experience on the island and could use an orgasm. As I pull down my panties, about to sit down, I feel his warm breath hit my ass and pussy and reflexively get up. He cries out in distress "please. Let me kiss your bot and vagene?" Yeah, he wants to be punished for selling out his people in support of Blackstone. Disparaging other people of color as sandcels, ricecels, nigcels and beancels, while literally kissing the asshole of the White Chad. Yes, I'm a girl of great privileged and I can do what I please with this incel piece of shit. Their bigotry far outweighs the exploitative nature of this venue.

What am I turning into? And besides incels of color are still people of color. Maybe if it was one of those Nazi stormcels, the worst of the worst. I look over the panel and find out you can select incels to use. They don't have pictures but only cartoon frog avatars, a brief description about them, and a ranking with the more virginal and extreme their ideology the more expensive they are to use. Luckily, I can't find Max. That would be horrific if Zach actually knew he selected a person of color. Maybe it was some nerdy Indian guy he bullied. It's a cruel world we live in.

Oh, here's one I'll select. Currycel500 descends back down into the abyss. A few minutes later another guy emerges. Yes, I recognize him. He's that stormcel who created a hierarchy of sexual desirability based on ethnicity, he even condoned the atrocities of the Aesthetic Revolution, and his avatar was of the cartoon toad peeing on a racist caricature of an African American.

I got to pee anyways. I know. I'll go on his face and then have him lick me clean. That'll teach him a lesson. But you have no idea the backstory of this person. What they've gone through. They once had a life with their own dreams just like you had as Max. But the bullying and alienation they experienced crushed those dreams turning them into a fascist.

You mustn't allow your privilege to cause you to dehumanize someone just because they posted something insensitive online. These privileged girls did the very same to Max for some of the shit he posted on the incel forums. Suddenly the room goes dark. I can't see anything. Must have been a power outage caused by the complexity of the mechanisms of this establishment. Suddenly a spot-light shines upon me. I'm standing on a stage as Natalie Bloom looking out over an audience of men in tuxedos and women in evening gowns, applauding me at some award ceremony. I bow down as the audience throws roses upon me and the credits for the show and outro synthwave track plays.

Chapter 26: Mentalcel Purgatory

As soon as the credits are over, I find myself awake and back in the examination room. I grab my hardon. I'm Max again.

Meschel says "even as a hot chick you'll always be a loser. But that's ok. It adds to the situational humor."

I look over at the screen and see Emma. She opens up the seat, sees an incel's face and then leaves with a look of shock and horror. Meschel notices my look of concern and laughs, "oh, how cute. You actually thought she'd go for a dweeb like you? I just fucking love taking an innocent young virgin like that and shocking her with the pure erotic essence of life. Her reaction alone makes me cum."

I'm relicved nothing physical happened to her but I still feel terrible that she was exposed to all this debauchery and exploitation. As I step outside I was expecting to see the Vaporwalk and Sea but I just see a parking lot at sunset and remember I was on the soundstage at Meschel's studio the entire time. When I get back to the Blackstone I check my phone.

I got a voicemail from my mom. She's crying, pleading:

"Max, please come home. We know all about the show. Your grandmother, she's stumbled upon that commercial of you attacking that poor woman and now she's in the hospital with a stroke. All our neighbors and family friends won't talk to us. We're complete social pariahs. I don't know what happened. Who convinced you to do this but I've got to say what you're doing is morally reprehensible and you need to come home now."

I put my head down on the pillow in shame. This isn't some ironic attempt at social commentary. No, this is just Hollywood taking the worst of human nature, the humiliation and dehumanization of others, and exploiting it for a quick buck. I get a beer from the minibar and try to calm down. I look over the incel forum to see what they think of the show. It seems that I have a cult following among them as they're embracing the character with my face as the new incel avatar rather than that cartoon toad.

One poster says that he's a locationcel because there are no aesthetically pleasing people where he lives and that we need to genocide the aesthetic proletariat so that he can finally get laid. Another says "why wagecuck and statusmaxx for a femcel who's also a 3 when I can just serve 10s in the seats. I'd rather get castrated and have to lick the sweaty assholes of 10s, the Chads and Stacies in the seats, then make love to an ugly foid and bring more worthless uglycels into this world."

One more says "Blackstone's not on our side. He's trying to convince us we'll benefit from his looks-based eugenics by just breeding more rich foids and Chads to mogg us. We're the real target here. They want to kill off all low status males. Let's eliminate them all first." One of them is going to snap, go on another rampage, and I'll have to live with that on my conscience.

Oh great Blackstone just officially came out against the show. He says "I absolutely disavow 'Max's Aesthetic World' and my campaign has nothing to do with this nonsense. My message is one of using aesthetics as a force of unity— uplifting all—regardless of age, race, religion, class, or creed. As for Max from the show. He was a trespasser on my property and I completely dissociate him from my campaign."

I break down in tears hearing Blackstone publicly disavow me. I truly have no prospects left. A social pariah for the rest of my life. I drink another beer and see if I can fall asleep. Just lying here in bed feeling this dark energy consume me. If I were to die right now, imagine all the horrors and torments that would await me for all eternity in the afterlife. Even though I'm not religious I feel like I'm already cursed to Hell. Trying to pray for atonement for everything I've done, but it just further triggers my OCD. Just try to meditate to clear out your mind. I feel myself falling, then I wake back up in a panic. I turn the lights on, take a few deep breaths, gulp down another beer, and then decide to head downstairs to go for a late night walk. Since it's a Friday, the shopping arcade is open late.

Looking at all the people, thinking about all the exploitation they're responsible for. No: that we're all responsible for. Our entire society is based upon the humiliation of others. Yes, from the service staff to the incels in the seats, all the social media followers, and of course the animals we exploit for food. And we're all told to just keep working and consuming to avoid any further humiliation as everyone who benefits goes on about their business like everything is fine. But it's not fine. I don't want to live in a world where someone like Ari Meschel can take an innocence girl like Emma and hurt her just for the profit and cheap thrills. This is just too ugly. No, this can't be our reality.

"We're all living in a simulation!" I shout. They just go on consuming, socializing with one another, living for the moment. Then I kneel down and start crying out at a world indifferent to these crimes. Some Chads walk by laughing, and one of them captures me crying on video.

Then two security guards approach me "Sir. You're going to have to leave the premises."

One does a facial scan with his phone and realizes who I am.

"Oh, you're on Meschel's tab. Please Sir, calm down," one says.

The other guard suggests I go over to the spa and get a message. I respond "I will not calm down. We need to take time to think about our impact on others, on this planet, and not just live for the pleasures of the senses." No, I've done too much thinking. Living in my thoughts instead of taking action. Maybe the guards are right. I apologize for my outburst and head back to my room.

I look over Blackstone's campaign website and notice he has revised his platform to be more inclusive, proposing platinum plans for all. Creating specialized versions for European Americans, Asian Americans, African Americans, Latinos, and Native Americans, tailored to each group's specific needs. Blackstone has also removed any reference to the aesthetics of the populace. He just talks about natalist policies for the middle and upper classes, incentivizing good urbanism, and of course funding for the arts, inclusive of all ethno-cultural and aesthetic preferences. As for immigration he wants a merit-based system but one that would select people using an algorithm favoring those who would make good citizens, compatible with a high trust society, rather than just human capital for corporations to exploit. It would probably be used to favor whites, but the change in tone is still probably smart on Blackstone's part. Just pray there's no more violence before the election.

I get my schedule. I have a shoot at the studio tomorrow, then the premier the day after, and then a week off. I'll decide whether it's worth going home or not. I return my mom's call. She keeps pleading in tears for me to stop the show and come home but I explain that I have no other choice and must do as they command, or they'll psychologically torture me out of existence. She says "I thought things through and I decided I'm not mad at you. They're taking advantage of your psychological state. We can sue them for that. Come home. Please."

She breaks down into tears. I try to assure her everything will be fine, but she hangs up on me.

I feel horrible but screw all those diagnoses. I'm no mentalcel. No, I'm the only one sane enough to see the world for what it is. I can see the path forward to the truth, where we need to go. My anxieties, depression, and frustrations are the side effects caused by the gatekeepers blocking my path forward. Just stuck, watching others be allowed to surpass me. Those who were granted the password, pre-destined to go forth from the moment of birth. That's why they want to numb great minds like mine so they can keep things as they are. Neutralize us so they can decide who gets to go forth. And that is exactly what this show is all about. Taking all the greatest creative potential and channeling it towards shit. Bored and still too anxious to sleep, I check back up on the incel forum. A new video, "Suicide fuel for prisoncels: what happens to incels in prison," has been posted.

I panic, knowing DCR's plans to create a punitive database of political dissidents, incels, sex pests, and social outcasts, and also Meschel's blackmail to use a deep fake to fabricate crimes against me and release my browsing history. After trying to avoid playing the video, my OCD causes me to click on it. There are references to Noam Metzenbaum in Connecticut, Toby Sharpe from the Dragon Day Massacre at Lockden University, the Aesthetic Revolution types, and then finally me for potentially inciting incel violence. About what would happen to us in prison. That because of the depiction of the Piñata Abortion scene, if I were to end up in prison the other inmates would declare me KOS, Kill on Site, as a baby killer. And that due to our small stature and boyish looks, we would face a fate worse than death, with the sadistic commenters speculating the grotesque details of how we'd finally lose our virginity. The man in the video mentions he saw some punk getting his wig split and cheeks busted in by an O.G. in prison just for downloading Loli from 4chan.

Shit, I have that Loli of Emma getting eaten out by a kangaroo saved to my hard drive. I lie in bed unable to sleep, envisioning those horrific scenarios, playing over and over in my head, and praying that Blackstone gets elected and uses the AI to make prisons safer rather than to monitor, track down, and send incels and dissidents there. Eventually I doze off and I find myself riding in the back seat of a car at night. I look out the window and it appears I'm driving down a remote highway in the middle of the desert. I look back and notice some sky-craft, a helicopter or drone, following the car.

"You're so fucked!" It's Delmont. "They're going to have a lot of fun with you," he adds.

I look out the window and notice we are approaching some town in the middle of the desert. We pull up to what appears to be an abandoned motel.

Delmont says "get out boy."

He drives off into the night and I'm stranded here alone in the motel parking. The sky craft now hovering over me. I walk over to the motel office to ask for help but it's deserted. Not a single car in the parking lot either. Suddenly I hear sirens and then several unmarked cars pull up in the parking lot. Men in all black with ski masks get out, yelling "down on the ground, hands behind your back!" Putting handcuffs on me, tossing me in the back of their trunk, and whisking me away to who knows where. My hands hurting, claustrophobic, with no idea of what's going on. Eventually I'm let out in what appears to be a black site prison in the middle of the desert. Some guards escort me into a concrete room and order me to strip. Once I'm stripped naked, two 7 foot tall female guards in Nazi-like uniforms inspect me. With a look of disgust, one female guard says "yeah, he's an incel." The other guard says "KOS."

The male guard adds: "the inmates have access to your entire search history. They know about the Loli." Then he orders me to walk down naked, with my hands still handcuffed behind my back, down a long dark corridor. I can hear shouting, and others screaming out in pain. I look to the side and see demonic looking creatures, with grotesque distorted faces behind the cages shouting, and trying to grab at me. I look

over and see an incel looking guy getting sodomized by the

creatures. Then in the next cell down, I see myself being

hacked to pieces.

Chapter 27: The Beverly Experience

It was just another bad dream. I get a text from Meschel, "that dream was really dark. We'll use it for an upcoming show. A Scared Straight for incels."

He reminds me we have a shoot today at the studio. I look in the bathroom mirror and notice a scar on the side of my head. Meschel must have had a chip implanted in my brain while I was tranquilized. Anyhow, the set for today certainly looks really cool. Of a seedy downtown area with a broken buzzing neon blade sign, very film noir.

On one side is a houseless man of color in front of a projected image of a houseless encampment and then there's a group of smug Chads in backwards blue Bluestone baseball caps, with their polo collars up to be super douchey. The DP instructs me to get into costume to be their chauffeur. Then orders us all to get in the limo. A video simulation on the windows makes it look like we're driving through some fictional city as I'm driving the Chads to a nightclub.

One of the Chads is instructed to tell me to pull over. They all get out and inspect a scruffy bearded houseless man of color.

The song "Drink da Pee" by "DJ Suck it Bitch" plays. I don't like the direction this is going. The Chads force the man down on his knees and order him to lean back with his head facing up. One of the Chads takes a urinal cake and places it on the man's face. The poor man pleads desperately to be left alone as they taunt and ridicule him. They all then proceed to urinate on the poor man's face. I inspect them closely. That's not simulated. That's real urine. Liquid waste of youth, privilege, and status upon the haggard face of crushed hopes and dreams.

The piss washing away the dirt and grime on his bearded face, revealing that he is in fact a White man. That feeling of relief that he's White? Class oppression is wrong regardless of the victim's race. As he's left aside to cry, drenched in piss, a jazz singer starts singing, "he's a poorcel, oh yes a poorcel and an oldcel, a middle-aged virgin without a penny to his name." When she's done singing some cops come over but not to apprehend the Chads but rather to arrest the houseless man.

Then the bulldozers crush the houseless encampment and knock over the old rundown buildings as everything goes dark. The blade sign turns back on but as the Bluestone Casino. Yes, dehumanize the underprivileged who are standing in the way of progress. Cool casino aesthetic though. Like something Blackstone would actually construct. But Blackstone seems like he actually wants to help people. Yes, he's a humanitarian. He just has an honest outlook on human nature.

Perhaps that's what's needed to reform the current order of business as usual. But this show is tarnishing his message by associating it with the worst of class oppression. I'm instructed to hold hands with Emma who is dressed like a Vegas showgirl to promote the new casino. We dance together to the lightshow. One romantic moment in this show of horrors. Then we all party at the casino's nightclub as the Chads take Emma away from me, grinding up against her. I should tell her how I feel tonight before it's too late.

Afterwards, while waiting outside, I see Meschel hand the houseless man a 20, refusing to let him use the restroom to wash the Chad piss off his face, and then yelling at him to scram. I feel so sick with myself. At this point if they want to release my browsing history, fine. Is there really anything they could reveal that's worse than this?

Meschel mentions something about celebrating at this new Asian Fusion place at Blackstone's Beverly Experience. The Experience was partially designed using an architectural algorithm, the first of its kind. Replicating the process of great architects of the past such as John C. Portman and John Jerde who designed casinos in Vegas and many 80s malls. We take several different cars, and Meschel coordinates it so Emma is with him and I'm kept separate in a car with some Chads.

It's a new automated parking structure so we can get off at the loading zone. I look up and admire the animated neon display of the exterior that has an Asian theme with lotus blossoms opening up and fire-spewing dragons. The neon outlined external glass escalator is really cool too, with the view looking out towards Downtown LA's skyline. I realize this is going to be a really magical location and it will be tough if I don't get with Emma as she's hanging out with the Chads. At the top of the escalator is a rotating sky lounge which has several corridors radiating out from it. We're informed to download the Beverly Experience app which will show us the direction to any establishment.

Part of the experience is wandering through the labyrinth of corridors which are constantly moving around within the confines of a giant puzzle box. A place to safely get lost. Until recently malls were all about utility. Minimalistic light and airy spaces with no sense of wonder or exploration. I look over and see Emma giggling with the Chads. You're still in the friendzone and those Chads move fast. And is she even morally ok with what happened today? All of them enjoying their lives to the fullest, with no guilt, remorse, or even an afterthought of what happened on the shoot.

I walk down a long corridor of shops through a glass tube that goes through a magical world of illuminated butterflies and flower blossoms. A perfume-like smell piped in too. I lost

sight of Emma and the Chads, distracted by the aesthetics, but

I download the app. There's a large central atrium that has a

network of glass tube elevators and escalators of neon of

various colors glowing in the dark. Different neon-lit

platforms moving up and down, rotating in circles and moving

horizontally and vertically, like a futuristic city in outer space.

The night sky full of glowing golden animated neon and

jewel-like bulb light fixtures that represent the crescent moon

and stars. I'm informed that every four hours the sky does a

full day's circle from sunset to sundown. Then as I'm looking

up, I notice what appears to be an island, illuminated like an

island of daylight resting upon a tower overlooking the atrium.

Yes, the restaurant. I take a glass tube escalator through the

illuminated turquoise colored misty clouds to that island in the

sky. Once the mist subsides, I arrive in the magical setting. A

grand entrance of stairs up to an Asian imperial palace,

clusters of pagodas alongside the cliffs, groves of cherry

blossoms and bonsai trees, and a waterfall that flows out and down into the atrium. I scan my app and a waitress escorts me to my seat. Through a cave that leads out to the dining area balconies overlooking the atrium. There's Meschel sitting right next to Emma and the Chads, surrounding her too.

I won't even be able to get a word in with her. Keeping it light, I just order a spicy tuna role and miso soup. I can't stand it any longer. Those Chads, talking about utter nonsense. They just know how to make the most asinine banter sound high status. Isn't that the key to everything? Leaving me out of the conversation. The one who actually met the man who made all this possible. Blackstone certainly values, or at least valued, my thoughts and ideas.

I look over the drink menu. Vaportinis made from Amazonian Vaporio, grown in sustainable vertical farms. Blackstone lied to me that Vaporio was only for elite consumption. Anyhow I order a mango Vaportini. The waitress asks me to sign an electronic waiver that says the Beverly Experience is not liable for any actions that occur under the influence of Vaporio. Just let the Vapor open up your intellect to Emma. Yes, I'll ask this: "Emma, are you speaking at the premier tomorrow?"

But Emma just responds in a loop, "oh, that's nice," over and over again. As the Chads keep making ape like noises. And Meschel too: "I'll give you a role if you let me eat your pussy," over and over again.

It's all nonsense. I can see things for what they are. I finish up my sushi and Vaportini and get up to go for a walk. As I walk through the restaurant, I notice the faces of the patrons are blurred yet I can see all the architectural aesthetics in such perfect detail. Up the spiral staircase to the top of the cliff where there is this really cool garden. Like being outdoors, perhaps in Japan in springtime with fragrant cherry blossoms and mist in the air. That giggling. I have to find where it's coming from.

Over the red arched bridge, over the waterfall which goes far down into the atrium. I follow the faint sound of giggling down a corridor, away from the main atrium. But the corridor is dark, like the remains of some abandoned section that was quarantined from the 80s. Perhaps from the original Beverly Center. The muted sound echoing in the distance, "Max, please help me," followed by giggling that gets creepier. A neon grid appears in the dark to show me the way. Turning various colors and disappearing behind me, constantly changing course. As the neon path ends, I reach a tall Jenga-like tower made of illuminated cubes of brick glass going way up into the dark sky. The cubes constantly moving, and changing color, with the lights turning on and off. From the base of the tower, I walk up a neon lit stairwell. Looking out, I see the glass cubes floating out into space. As I examine them closer, I notice each one contains a particular memory, some traumatic, some romantic. Some cry out in pain for their missed chance to come into fruition. While others taunt me about the opportunities I missed out on. I try to walk on to one where I see a long lost crush but each one just floats away into space. All my missed dreams, the many that didn't come into fruition. Each particular moment lost in that state for all eternity. Crying out at me as they float away into the abyss. I did this to them for not taking action and giving them a chance to bloom. The next glass cube is one of an old man on his death bed. I examine him closely. Is that my grandfather? The man mumbles to himself "I'm almost dead but I think about my life. The dreams I had in youth. It was all for shit." He notices me, "it's you! You fucked me. You could have made those dreams a reality if you weren't such a little pussy!" He then floats away stuck in that state of eternal regret. That was me in the future. Another one of Meschel's VR traps for the show. I've got to get the hell out of this simulation. I run back but I'm blocked. The gates closing in behind me.

That's how life works. How if you fail to move on to the next stage in life, you're permanently fucked with no turning back to correct you're mistakes and missed opportunities. What Blackstone said about how you have to backtrack in order to get to that path to a better future. What he said about achieving the power to transcend time and space and reclaim lost futures. Reclaiming the lost dreams of youth. But the reality is that we must go forward to face our fate, the reality that outside forces shape our destiny. The path beneath me is now dark, the neon stairwell is gone too, and I'm forced to walk inside the one last cube. I then try to step back outside but it looks like I'm trapped inside. I walk down a long hallway and I can hear Meschel talking to someone. At the end of the hallway is a large door.

Should I open the door and play dumb? Fuck Meschel. You don't owe him anything. As I channel my energy towards my hatred for Meschel and everything he stands for I feel my consciousness leaving my body, my perspective drifting past the doors and into a large conference room which overlooks Downtown LA. I look down from the top of the door frame so that I'm looking down at Meschel and his conversation partner.

"DCR is still confident he'll win this thing," says the man. He's a slim, well-groomed, racially ambiguous looking man in a slim fit suit.

"But the amount of support Blackstone is generating," he continues, "particularly among young men could be a huge problem, if not this election cycle than during the next one."

"What we need to start doing is thinking like Blackstone," says Meschel. "We need to convert his Revolutionary message into something totally harmless to us. We need to create a politics which appropriates Blackstone's aesthetics that these incel losers love so much as well as his Basic-Income type policies. I don't know if it's advisable to give these creeps cash and the choice of what to spend it on, but I definitely think very basic housing and food could be arranged. It wouldn't have to be anything fit for a dog, mind you. I don't think they'd complain. I mean who cares if you're living in a pod sustained only by soylent if you're hooked up to a VR simulation all day? These people are easily led and neutered. Just look how sheep-like they are in their following of Blackstone. Anyway, I'm confident a combination of the VR-programing I'm developing with DCR's basic housing and food is the best way to keep these people's nascent political energies perfectly quelled and sublimated. Blackstone says

that true freedom is the ability to live in the utopia you desire?

Well I'll be damned if we don't give it to em! They'll be able

to live where they want and fuck who they want but it will all

be fake."

So, this is the end-game of the show. I knew it couldn't just all

be about money, that there was some kind of ulterior motive

and an outside hand involved. I must find some way to get the

truth out there.

I drift back into my body and find myself in what appears to

be a maintenance corridor of the Beverly Experience, but

everything is dark. Too dark to see, but that crying. I run down

the corridor, chasing that voice which leads me to a tiny door.

It's locked but I'm able to use the Beverly Experience app to

open it. Inside is a lavishly furnished doll house. Large enough

for me to fit inside. At a table set for tea is a series of dolls, an

Emma the Nature Girl action figure, one of me, and then one

that is really strange. Naked, and damaged like someone did

some occultist experiment. As I'm inspecting the strange doll, something startles me. The doll is crying, its face animated like it's alive. I inspect it closely. It looks like Natalie Bloom. The Natalie doll turns to me and cries out "Max, save me from the Vapor!" I close my eyes and put my hands on my face to see if there's any VR set.

When I open my eyes, I find myself curled up in a fetal position, inside of a large dollhouse at a high-end toy store. Some woman with her small daughter notices me and says "security! There's a creep talking to himself inside the dollhouse."

I scream at her "I sexually identify as a doll you bigoted cunt!" The woman is dumbfounded. I examine the dolls closely again. They're all merchandise for the show. Even the Natalie doll. But that wasn't part of the show. I Remember what Blackstone said about saving Natalie from the Vapor. I run outside the store and sit alongside the fountain and try to calm down. Perhaps this was just a bad trip from that Vaportini? It's daytime now back at the atrium with the giant sun themed astronomical clock as the centerpiece. Verdant hanging gardens alongside the atrium.

I find my way back to the restaurant but discover they have all left without me. I run off, devastated, taking the glass elevator down to the very bottom. At the lowest level the elevator emerges on a platform which is surrounded by glass barriers against the body of water that the waterfall flows into. I look up and see that the ground floor of the atrium is actually above the water level. There's even a gondola boat ride you can take through a grotto. Down another corridor is the entrance to the recently opened Metro station. There's a deal with Metro that accepts Blackstone credits from my app. From there I take the new Metro Pink Line and transfer at the Wilshire/La Cienega station, then take the Purple Line to the Wilshire/Rodeo Station where there's an underground passageway connecting to the Blackstone. The Beverly Experience was an experience indeed.

Chapter 28: The Premiere

Today is the premiere of the show. When everything I so feared is presented to respectable society. My family, all past acquaintances, the media, and millions of strangers. I've gotten a text that says to meet Meschel at his office for a briefing before the premiere. He owns you, remember?

After I get ready, a chauffeur is waiting for me at the loading zone to take me to Meschel's studio in Culver City. At the studio I can already see the big crowds around the gate. They can't see me through the tinted windows but there's a group of girls in anime cosplay holding signs saying "we love you Max." Maybe I was wrong to doubt this. Fame and status await if you just play the role. I'm escorted over to Meschel's office. Meschel says "this is a big premiere. We have huge excited crowds, but the situation is volatile. This is where I need your help."

"You do?" I respond.

Meschel says "Max, don't think of this as a burden. You have an opportunity to be part of something greater than us all. Those incels out there. They're not just online anymore. Many of them, claiming to be inspired by you have purchased tickets to cause trouble for the show, with many more driving in from all over the nation to stage an insurrection against the Hollywood elites who they blame for their predicament. The Aesthetic Revolution is also likely in attendance. They're a lot better organized then those incels and could do serious damage. This is where you come in, Max. Those incels view you as their hero. Someone fighting for their rights. They'll listen to you so I need you to de-escalate the situation. Give a speech at the premier and tell them to knock off all the crazy shit. Make the case that their lives are being enriched by consuming. That their sexual market value will increase by purchasing our merchandise. And the press is there too, along with protesters including antifa. The press insists we're contributing to the toxic climate and possibly inciting incels and fascists. Tell them all that we're an entertainment venue and don't endorse any political ideologies. And the antifa. They think we're complacent in all this and have threatened to riot if we don't explicitly denounce bigotry. Tell them we're donating 5% of our proceeds to fighting hate. But you need to be careful not to alienate the incel base either."

I look at him in confusion. Meschel says "relax, we're just all about the spectacle. You understand?"

I nod in agreement. Shortly afterwards I head over to the Irv Meschel Auditorium for the screening. The auditorium was named for Meschel's father, Irv, who directed some raunchy sex comedies back in the 80s.

The plaza in front of the auditorium is swarmed with crowds, many climbing over the fence or running past the police barricade, with lots of drones and choppers hovering up above. There's a large group of Blackstone supporters, not all incels. There's the preppy fashy Chads in purple Blackstone baseball caps, and then the manbun wearing Woke Chads and lots of normies. Fans who don't necessarily support Blackstone but appreciate the show for its satire. And of course: the masses of incels. Some ugly, almost like Hollywood caricatures of incels but many just look like healthy normal young men of all ethnic and social backgrounds. These people think the show gives them a voice, a cultural space, and even some degree of status.

Many wearing the old school frog masks and many more with masks of my face. There's a short scrawny LatinX guy with a "Hug a Tacocel" sign and an overweight African American guy holding a sign, "Blackcels for Blackstone: Down with Chad & Tyrone." And then there's the stormcels who look like they might be with the Aesthetic Revolution. And of course: the counter-protesters. The trust fund brats from Beverly Hills Antifa, women with feminist slogans protesting incels, and a ragtag assortment of angry leftists. One woman holding a sign saying "you incels want eugenics? Why don't you start with yourselves." Others with signs accusing incels of color of being complacent with White Supremacy.

As I walk past the plaza to the screening, the incels notice me. They all form a line with each incel taking turns, bowing, paying their respects to me as their leader. I'd feel terrible letting them down, knowing the endgame of Meschel and elite interests behind this to turn another generation of young men into zombies. When I enter the auditorium, I notice the attendees having to go through a facial recognition scan to screen out incels. The idea that you can categorize someone based on how they look for social exclusion. I thought we've moved beyond that. I'm escorted inside to sit at the very front with Meschel, the rest of the cast, the studio executives and other bigshots financing all this. Meschel gets up on stage,

"Welcome everyone. I'm excited to announce the premier of Max's Aesthetic World. We have a fantastic show for you today. But before we begin, a special treat. The star of Max's Aesthetic World, Max von Mueller."

I'm cued to walk up on stage to a round of applause. Meschel pulls me in for a tight hug, his head touching my chest, and his breath smelling of booze.

"Don't fuck this up," he warns.

I remember what he said. About how this is all just for entertainment value and that it stands for nothing. I look out at the audience, the stuck up Chadsworth students, the media gatekeepers, and all the other rich people financing the show. And there's Emma too. She's charming as usual but something seems off. Stop making eye contact with them. No, pretend they're naked. You don't want to get a boner. Just take a deep breath in and try not to make eye contact. I just got a text from Meschel,

"What are you waiting for. Just play off your own quirky humor."

I take the mic,

"Hi guys," I say in an awkward strained voice, "it's a pleasure being with you today and you all seem like really kind people."

The audience. They're snickering and sneering at me.

Fuck them. I start, "this show……this show has no vision."

The audience gasps in shock. I continue "It exploits and appropriates the culture of those who were never given a place in society, turning their alienation, pain, and humiliation into an object of ridicule for entertainment." Now Meschel looks like he's about to strangle me.

I continue, "their dreams, no, our dreams are being exploited by those who know how to play the game but don't have the vision. We dream it but they get to live in it. We deserve a place at the table. No, we deserve to set the agenda here. We're not just incels. No, we're the artist, the dreamer, the intellectual, the innovator. The gatekeepers discard our visions. And if we manage to get one through, they just exploit them, turning them to shit for profit. But this ends here. We are not going to be exploited any longer! Listen to Blackstone. He actually wants to take inspiration from the best thinkers and implement those visions to advance civilization. But this show? It's just like masturbation. Yeah, it can be fun but it's accomplishing nothing. And to all you incels and Aesthetic Revolution types out there who think Meschel's on your side:

He's not. I overheard him myself. It's an organon of social control to mute your energy. He wants to suck you all up into a VR simulation and have you living in pods and eating shit. He's in league with DCR's campaign, operating specifically to counter Blackstone."

The mic is shut off so I can't continue. At this point I've set my destiny for better or worse. There's no turning back from this now. Pacing back and forth, I look out at the audience, the press, and studio executives. I am so fucked. No matter what I do it's over for me. Suddenly I hear a bang. The door is pushed open, with young men rushing in from outside. The first wave of men in frog masks screeching autistically. Then another wave of men who were plants in the audience put on their purple Blackstone baseball caps. Fashy bodybuilders, those handsome enough to make it passed the lookist facial scan. I put my hand up in a fist to show solidarity, chanting, "Hail Blackstone! Hail our Aesthetic Utopia!" The Aesthetic Revolution Guys Roman salute me back. But things are about to get ugly. One of the incels punches out some frail-looking wealthy older investor and I hear screaming. People trying to escape, but the incels have blocked the way out.

Meschel shouts "Max, shut this all down!"

A bunch of men start pummeling Meschel. Another group of incels start attacking a female studio exec, stripping off her clothes, and bitch slapping her across the face as they chant, "death to gatekeepers!" Then the incels in frog masks start awkwardly rubbing up against the Chadsworth students who are hovering into a corner with cringe expressions. And then there's Emma. I really hope she's ok. She's looking at me to rescue her. Now's my chance to be a white knight. I turn to the incels, "leave her alone."

Some of the Chadsworth guys turn to me, with one saying, "Blackstone's cool bro." The incels back away from the Chadsworth girls as the Chads start chanting, "Blackstone!" over and over. Then one nerdy Beverly guy whines, "Blackstone's a Nazi. I like DCR." The other Chads ignore him, cheering on as the incels beat up Meschel and the other studio executives, investors, and journalists. One guy who must have hacked into the loudspeaker plays some fashwave. The Chads take it as an opportunity to take off their polos and start grinding up against the girls. The incels look pissed. One incel screeches, "you richfags don't support our cause. You're just bored with having everything and want an excuse to rebel!" The Chads ignore him and start making out with the girls as the incels just fondle themselves to the spectacle from the sidelines. One female journalist, panicking frantically, as she obsessively says #MeToo over and over.

"Police! Open up!"

When the police show up they'll probably arrest me and Meschel will spin it to make me culpable for all this. Using a deep fake to fabricate more crimes of a nature that will almost certainly guarantee inhumane treatment in prison. An event the media will hype to tarnish Blackstone, further associating him with both loserdom and fascist tyranny. Some guys from the Aesthetic Revolution surround me. One guy says, "Max, we've got the door covered but you've got to escape." They direct me to behind the stage where there's an escape route.

The police say "this is your final warning! We're coming in!"

I enter through the emergency escape which leads through to the network of maintenance hallways. I am the first to walk through and the incels and Aesthetic Revolution follow me. One guy mentions "we hacked into Meschel's system and found the way out."

Running through the maintenance hallway, men in white lab coats run frantically out of our way. As we near the exit, I remember there's something I still need to do. I remember Meschel's VR lab just around the corner, and what Blackstone said about rescuing Natalie from the vapor. I have to find her and set everything right with Blackstone. She is the girl so beautiful and righteous that she will set order in the cosmos and usher in a new millennium of peace, justice, and aesthetic perfection.

I stop short as the incels and Aesthetic revolution pile out of the exit to freedom. I make my way back down the hallway to an adjoining passage, working as much off of my hazy memories of the day I was transformed into Natalie Bloom, as the gut instincts Blackstone promised me would kick in at the crucial time of action. I find the VR lab, and as if by some miracle it is unlocked and empty. All of Meschel's white-coat stooges must have split the moment security was breached. I see the chair with a VR headset and Vaporio IV drip. Knowing what I must do, I slip the needle into my arm, and the headset onto my face…

I awake in a bed inside a small cabin. Perhaps on a ship. Wait, a ship? No, I get motion sickness. I get out of bed and rush down a long narrow hallway. Yes, must be a cruise ship.

"Help, please help," faint crying echoing out in the distance.

At the end of the hallway is a large banquet hall. Exquisite, like one of those old Ocean Liners, perhaps the Queen Mary or Titanic. It's all deserted, but that odor. Large tables lined with the finest china, filled with…wait what? Decapitated heads, not decomposing but freshly removed. All my old

rivals, everyone I felt snubbed by or who disrespected me in

adolescence. From images I posted of them to the incel forum.

"Don't you love it? I did this all for you."

I look up and see a nerdy young man in an orange prison

jumpsuit inside a cage hanging from the ceiling. It must be

Noam, but is it really him? Then I look at all the heads in

disgust, realizing that I'm too soft hearted to be a killer.

"Aren't you in prison?" I ask.

Noam says "father made a deal so I could serve out my

sentence here in the Vapor. Once I'm released all my visions

shall be implemented and I shall rule over this wretched race

of beings."

"Your dad is Roger Blackstone?" I ask.

Noam says "he felt bad about abandoning my mother and I so

he handed me the keys to the Vapor."

Noticing I'm about to leave, Noam says "you're going to need that," pointing to a katana sword next to the heads.

He adds "I used it to decapitate my adversaries. It's yours to save the princess."

I thank him, grab the katana, and quickly rush past the banquet hall and to the ship's main atrium.

"Please, help," I hear the voice getting louder.

I climb up a spiral staircase and find myself on the deck of the ship in a rainstorm. There she is: Natalie Bloom. Naked and tied to the base of the ship's smoke-stack. Crying with duct tape over her mouth but unable to make eye contact with me. All her smooth pale skin, and her nice golden bush. No, don't look at her like that in a moment like this.

I feel a tap on my back. It's Meschel, with a captain's hat, an open Hawaiian shirt exposing his hairy chest, and smoking a cigar. Meschel says snickering, "enjoying the cruise? It's your consolation prize now that we no longer need you for the show."

"I'm done with your games," I protest.

Meschel says "you really thought you could fuck with me?

Remember I own you? And with the new deep-fake I can do

anything with your image, and you can go back to being a

pathetic, unemployable, incel. And to think you could have

had it all, money, fame, and pussy."

"Whatever, just let the girl go," I plead. Meschel responds:

"white knighting for a figment of your imagination? How

pathetic. You know there's millions of guys right now on the

Meschel Vision stream bidding on what happens to this poor

innocent maiden."

"Oh, here's one," Meschel adds looking over his phone,

"Cover Natalie in a bucket of deadly poisonous sea slugs."

Meschel laughs hysterically as a shipmate walks over carrying

a big bucket of sea slugs. Then he starts caressing Natalie.

When he's distracted, I ram the katana right into his stomach.

Suddenly I hear a loud bang. Meschel says "you really don't

get it. This isn't some lucid dream. Your actions here have

real-life repercussions." I notice the ship is starting to sink so I untie Natalie, quickly grab her, and jump on the nearest life-boat. Meschel still screaming out "I still own you! I own the girl! I own it all!" The ocean finally reaches the deck of the ship and we drift out to sea.

Chapter 29: The Perfect Movie Ending

I find myself on a pink paddle boat on a calm body of water surrounded by rolling golden hills and groves of oaks. It's golden hour, the late afternoon sun highlighting the reflections upon the lake and natural surroundings. This must be near my old home in the Bay Area. Yes, I recognize the iconic tower of the Lafayette Reservoir where I'd often go hiking, and the sound of geese.

I wonder if I fell asleep here and all those wild adventures were just some long, crazy dream or something to do with the VR. No sign of Natalie either. I put my hand in the water. The contrast in temperature of the cool water and warm dry air, and the natural scents too. No way, this is part of the simulation. Oh great. There's a helicopter zooming towards me. The police must be looking for me after all that went down at Meschel's studio. I burry my head in my lap and close my eyes, hyperventilating.

"Max, get in!" I look up and see two guys from the Aesthetic Revolution letting down a rope ladder for me to climb up. Once I get onboard, the guys explain that Blackstone is having a fundraiser at a mansion nearby in Orinda. The guys give me a mask depicting my own face, from the show. I'm informed I'm probably on the do not admit list, and thus need a disguise. The view from the helicopter is superb. Looking down over the reservoir, the glistening golden hills, woodlands, and clusters of wealthy residential areas, San Pablo and Briones reservoir in the distance, and then out to the fog shrouded East Bay Hills. The chopper starts to descend over a mansion, nestled in a eucalyptus grove on a hillside where I notice a large gathering. As we get closer, I can tell the people aren't expecting us.

The Aesthetic Revolution guys assist me down with the rope ladder to where I'm surrounded by a crowd of well-dressed attendees who are giving me curious looks.

I'm informed that Blackstone is using this fundraiser to reveal a pilot program for his pan-enclavist vision for California, proposing a public/private partnership with his real estate firm to foster building projects to celebrate diversity in the Bay Area, with architectural scale models of plans for Americana and European-inspired developments in nearby towns in Contra Costa County and other projects to celebrate Chicano, Afro-futurist, Chinese, and Hindu heritage throughout the Bay Area.

Despite this grand celebration of diversity, those around me appear to be those of wealth and privilege: well-dressed in the finest retro Italian suits and aviator sunglasses, the fashion of a new Future Fash counter elite rather than the usual business casual attire of Silicon Valley. Lots of preppy blonde teens in Chadsworth Alamo uniforms; they're grooming the youth of the local elite I suppose.

There's no overtly stereotypical incels and no sign of the Aesthetic Revolution either. Those without status and little to lose are always the vanguard and then cast aside for the new elite to rise. Blackstone certainly doesn't want to be associated with the incels and their bad optics. Two of Blackstone's private security detail apprehend me, ordering me to remove my mask. When they find out who I am they explain that I have to come with them.

The guards escort me to a cabin-like guest house where I find Roger Blackstone lounging on a sofa, sipping sake. Blackstone starts by making small talk about how he's kind of a recluse at these events. I just smile, feeling a bit awkward. Not like that night when we shared a special bond and I discovered the secrets of the Universe.

"Max, do you realize what you've accomplished?" He proclaims. I don't know what to say.

Blackstone explains "at first I was unhappy with the show and all but you just did me a huge favor. Did you hear that Meschel was just arrested? One of his #MeToo accusers was inspired to press charges after your speech. The cops also found a naked young man who told them he was being kept as a sex slave in some horrid chamber beneath the studio. This means we can go forth with the lawsuit."

Blackstone offers me a sake and further explains, "one of my programmers for Blackstone Inc. was simultaneously working for the adult VR site COOMTUBE. I fired him for breaching contract by working there. Out of spite he handed over top secret technology from Vapor Vision over to Meschel. But now that Meschel is facing serious criminal charges we can go forth with the lawsuit and have a very strong case."

"Where do I come into this?" I ask.

Blackstone explains "I am re-launching the Vapor Vision VR entertainment to give the masses a taste of what it's like to be able to live in one's own utopia, except unlike with Meschel's it will be a preview for what's to come. Due to the controversy with the show I can't have you front and center, but I'd like you to help with the aesthetic components of the project behind the scenes." With Meschel out of the picture and Blackstone wanting to collaborate with me. This is it. That once in a lifetime golden ticket to the good life.

Blackstone lets me crash here at the guest house and in the morning arranges for me to take an Uber back to Modesto. When I arrive home my family rushes up to hug me. My mom is in tears and my dad has also been worried sick. Even Stacey gives me a big hug. They don't even grill me about the show. They're just happy to have me back. I spend the next week relaxing, catching up on online news and forum postings, and I even try playing golf. I explain to my family about the internship with Blackstone and they're all thrilled for me. They've even rethought their opinion of Blackstone himself now that he's modified his views, and he's now almost tied with DCR in the polls.

I finally get a text from Blackstone's assistant, arranging plans. With enough time to pack, Blackstone hails an Uber to take me back to the Bay Area. I'm dropped off to meet Blackstone at his new studio space in Dublin. It's a warehouse type structure in an office park. I'm escorted by a staff member to Blackstone's office where he's ecstatic with more great news.

Blackstone explains that Meschel's attorneys have agreed to hand over full control of the software to Blackstone Inc. under the condition that I agree to sign a non-disclosure agreement about everything I experienced on the show and related social events. Blackstone mentions that the tabloids released a photo of the socialite daughter of a prominent billionaire sitting on the toilet with a guy's face peeking out from underneath her and now there are conspiracy theorists spreading rumors about #Seatgate: that Meschel is part of some secret society to blackmail the wealthy and powerful with footage of their offspring engaged in debauched acts and that he too was being blackmailed by shady elite interests.

Blackstone explains that I'll be his intern for cultural and aesthetic research for the VR program. I'm given a tour of the studio and meet the team who I'll be working with. Blackstone explains that there's an apartment within the studio for me to stay and even a gourmet food court, pool, and gym. I get to do what I love, researching aesthetic imagery online, and brainstorming ideas for VR with the team.

A week later over Labor Day weekend is the grand opening of Blackstone's Oasis Resort in Alamo. As we approach the resort from the car, I notice a collection of ski-lodge-like structures nestled in the foothills of Mount Diablo. We drive past an exclusive residential area and then through the main gate to where a valet escorts us from the loading zone. There's a grass lawn in front and an area of pine and oaks surrounding the complex. We walk through the grand entrance, past a manmade waterfall fountain, and under a tasteful animated bulb sign which has yet to be lit up.

The warm dry air is fragrant with wood from the structure, natural scents of grass and pine, chlorine from the waterfall, and a hint of perfume and various sweets. Amongst the mountain-lodge-like structure, the waterfall pours into a creek that meanders throughout the complex, with wooden bridges over the water, and a giant waterwheel. There's even a wooden skybridge connecting to the hotel tower which has an external glass elevator and an alpine themed astronomical clock. Beyond the hotel complex, the creek flows out into a woodland area forming a small lake with water aerating up into the air.

I can see Mount Diablo and the foothills glistening in gold as it approaches sunset. There's even a lazy river, for patrons to swim in, that goes into the oak woodlands and small canyon. After a brief tour, I head over to the concert area where the event is being held on a wood podium overlooking the lake, with lanterns that reflect upon it. Just savoring the moment, looking out over the water features at sunset, as all kinds of celebrities and prominent figures pose for photo ops. Blackstone has risen in the polls, with many elites and people of status becoming seduced by his aesthetics. The press and attendees even want photo-ops with me. It's good that the show didn't turn me into a total social pariah. Fame is a valuable currency regardless, but I'm sure glad I've moved on to more constructive endeavors.

That giggling? I turn around and notice that Blackstone is talking to two pretty young blonde girls. It is Emma and wait, Natalie Bloom too? Emma notices me and gives me a big hug.

She mentions something about modeling at the resort and that she will be attending Chadsworth Alamo for her senior year. Emma introduces the girl as Adrian, her friend from Chadsworth Alamo. I examine Adrian closely, and am almost certain that she is Natalie Bloom.

I turn to Blackstone: "Natalie Bloom, is it her?"

Blackstone feigns confusion, but then looks at Adrian longingly, and there's a golden sparkle in his eye. Then I glance over at Emma. Emma smiles back at me. There's an aura that everything is back to the dreams I had in the naivety of youth, that anything is possible, and my senses are alive, heightened with full intensity. Just like in my original vision of the oasis. Emma suggests we all go to the lazy river for a swim. I follow her into the magic of the night, and, just briefly, feel like I've finally tapped into it: the current which weaves together romance, aesthetics—all that constitutes man's longing to be re-united with the Divine—into a perfect balance and harmony.